THE SH.

IMP AND THE BEAST

STEPHANIE HUDSON

THE SHADOW IMP SERIES

To Jess,

IMP AND THE BEAST

Happy Reading :)

Stephenie

Imp and the Beast
The Shadow Imp Series #1
Copyright © 2021 Stephanie Hudson
Published by Hudson Indie Ink
www.hudsonindieink.com

Imp and the Beast/Stephanie Hudson – 1st ed.
ISBN-13 - 978-1-913904-96-8

In true Pip fashion I decided to ask my kids what they would dedicate the books to. So here is my daughter Ava's dedication.

I dedicate this book to all Zombies. I am not sure what to thank you for but I guess if I had to choose it would be... Thank you for not eating us.

STEPHANIE HUDSON

WARNING

This book may or may not but most likely does..okay, so it definitely does contain content of a sexual nature. Now if the idea of monster sex makes you want to go screaming into the night as you make the sign of the cross, then this book probably isn't the best choice for you. However if you have raised a brow with intrigue, then I welcome you to this sinful goodness.

So get yourself comfortable, and strap in, as you're in for a bumpy, fun filled, naughty ride.

Love Pip.

Your friendly neighbourhood Imp.

STEPHANIE HUDSON

ONE

MY BAD

"Haha, Gotcha!" I shouted with utter joy at beating my latest foe... sneaky little bastard couldn't escape my genius, or my rainbow glitter flip flop for that matter. Of course, the battle wasn't over as the little bulgy eyed bugger had a comrade, one that now wanted to get his revenge for me squishing his friend.

"Wah you doing, Aunty Pippy?" the sweetest voice in the world asked from behind where I was balancing on a pair of rare late-17th century walnut chairs. They were English, and what was known in the fussy fart of the antique world as the William and Mary period, circa 1695.

I mean, how jammy is that? Born into royalty and then have an era of furniture making, one you had nothing to do with, named after you!

Not that I was bitter, of course, because unlike these silver-spooned bloomers, I had contributed in other ways to the Western world. But oh no, that list would have been classed as bragging. Like the time I introduced my buddy Leo to Lisa del Giocondo, better known as Mona Lisa, who just so happened to become the most recognised painting in history. Or like when I invented the word *Dude* back in the 1870's, no one thought it was going to catch on in replacing the word dandy, but yet here we are now and it's still going strong. Take that, Shakespeare. I mean, okay, so the dude (see what I did there) did invent like a bazillion words in the English language, but come on, 'fishify', what was he thinking with that one!? Now, as for Wittolly and Zany, now those were the Shanizzle!

But that's getting way off the bug killing topic, and well, I was barely on it to begin with before my mind led me down the fancy chair route. At this point, I should probably mention that I kinda suffer from what I like to call Squirrel syndrome… thank you Pixar's movie UP for that little beauty. Basically, for those who haven't seen this

ECC (Epic Cuteness Classic), it's when the dogs are all talking and then suddenly stop as they smell a squirrel. Well, this is like me and my brain. We don't always get along... and yes, I know what you're thinking, *is this chick mental?* And the answer would be a possible yes, what I tell people is a definite no.

Truth is I was just... Me.

Uniquely unique.

Like the comforting butter you want on a sandwich even when your filling is wet and you don't need it, because your bread isn't dry and you can't even taste it... but, like I said, it's comforting, so you spread me anyway. Now was this madness...? To some brainy dude with glasses, potentially so... but to those who know me, I'm just spreadable fat you want to lick off your finger or smother over your baked potato.

So, getting away from butter and back to the question...

"I'm catching flies, sweet pea, peach, pear, plum," I said, knowing she would giggle at her long-winded name that was always worth it in my mind. Of course, everything I said was usually long winded but geez, those crazy looks I get made it totally worth it! But my complete and utter favourites were the warm, lovely big ones I got from my snuggle bun cake…

My Adam.

He was the Joker to my Harley Quinn, the Mulder to my Scully, the Bert to my Ernie, the iron to my Man… err, wait, not sure that one works, but hey you get the idea here. Adam was my everything! Of course, he also was the most powerful being in all the Realms combined, but to me, he was simply my squishems.

Now of course, it wasn't always like this, as at one time I was meant to be a crunchy little snack for the big guy, hulk side of Adam, but that was until he got to know me, and realised sometimes even food could be entertaining… and not in a 'hey look this apple is cut into the shape of a bird' way, which I could totally do. Now, making a bird apple fly was another thing entirely, as throwing it off the top of Afterlife didn't exactly go well, especially not when it fell on the roof of a Ferrari that the King of Kings had been getting into at the time. Let's just say that shit like that was kinda my calling card, so it didn't take a genius to know who the culprit was. But then, that's when my buddy, pal and spawn of my best friend's loins comes in handy, as I seem to be able to get away with a lot more stuff if I have my small companion with me.

Of course, she was as cute as a button... although, why anyone ever called buttons cute, is beyond even my brand of crazy... but she was my little buddy, who became my excuse for, well... pretty much everything I did, as I never failed to entertain her.

But I am getting way ahead of myself, because you could be reading this and be like... wait, what... I have no kumquat of an idea what this green and blue haired chick's on about.

Well, let me give you the low down on this high jacked up story narrative.

My name's Winifred Pipper Ambrogetti... I know, I know, mouthful, right, plus Winifred... what Momma tree was even thinking with that one, I will never know. Jeepers, even Pocahontas' parents could have come up with something better for this mad chica! Now though, Pip suits me just fine and it's what most people call me. As for what I look like, well nobody wants to read half of a bloody story without knowing what the main characters looks like now, do they...? Nope, that shit pisses me off, because I think in my head, yeah, they look bitchin' hot with hot pink hair and then boom! They got brown... nope, that shit don't fly with this narrator.

So, quick rundown, my hair's green with blue tips, and thank the breezy for hair dye was all I can say, 'cause that henna crap was not fun. Plus, it smelled like rotting cabbage! You could say that there was a reason one of the worst jobs in history was done by the dudes that dyed shit purple, and why purple was a royal colour... because it was expensive for a reason. Created from the desiccated glands of sea snails, those poor buggers were smashed open and dried out in the sun before being boiled and left fermenting for ten days before even a single small swatch of fabric could be turned purple. Those snails became more expensive than gold, and what made this one of the worst jobs ever, was you were basically committing yourself to becoming the smelliest person in the town, and that shit stank worse than shit itself!

But again, this feels like another squirrel moment, so moving on once more...

My big eyes are green with a ring of blue, hence the matching hair, which so far, I hadn't gotten bored of. Now, if you were to ask me what my natural colour was, then the answer to that secret would be red. I know, shocker right. As for my features and shit, well I was classed as cute. I'm talking seriously cute here, not beautiful, even if Adam told me I was… and daily.

But, thanks to my dimples, I think the word was more childlike and due to my non-existent height, then I was often mistaken for one, which is eww when you're kissing your hubby. But then I didn't exactly help matters wearing kid's clothes, which were so much cooler than those stuffy adult fashions that basically covered what I classed as way too much skin.

But then, I never cared much for what people thought of me, so I basically wore whatever the hell's bells I wanted. Which was also why I was tattooed and had multiple piercings, including, lip, nose, tongue, a bunch in my ears, belly button and well, an even more fun place that Adam adored as it had his name written there in the tiniest of letters around a ring of gold. It was even more fun whenever he tugged at it with his teeth and growled at me.

But then this wasn't the only place I liked to display my devotion to my husband, as I also had his name tattooed over my knuckles surrounded by hearts and flowers. Something I had surprised him with one anniversary. Now, like I said, I suffered a bit in the height department, which may or may not be classed as a disadvantage but hey, that's what heels were invented for, right? I mean men wore heels for years to make them look taller because, well, back then six foot was classed as giant tall. But like I said, I don't need to go into any details on just how short my ass was, only that it was less than five large feet but way more than five baby feet.

I was also skinny, with just a little handful of boobs that didn't need a bra, and hips that flared out enough that shit didn't just fall down. I also had what Adam called a peach bum and heart shaped lips... the ones on my face not my front bum, hehe. Now, I could go into more detail, but I guess there was a reason people never described what their feet looked like in books, because, well, even I knew what TMI meant. But if not, then my feet were bitchin'... *just saying.*

Now, as for my bitchin' style, well, I was what most would consider a trend setter and if they didn't, then they were fools because, hello, my style killed all other styles in an EDB (Epic Death Battle). Basically, this translates into wearing whatever the hell I want. Like now, I'm wearing awesome dungarees I made from an old patchwork quilt I bought at a market in Hamilton, Missouri, which is basically the quilting capital of the World!

I mean I was never planning on putting that shit on my bed, and it wasn't like I had a rocking chair... oooh, mental list, buy rocking chair and paint... lots and lots of paint.

But, back to now and wearing my super comfy, padded, patchwork dungaree shorts with only one strap buckled. Under these, I wore tights that looked like the legs of Sally from Nightmare before Christmas, one of my favy films. I also wore monster feet slippers and a t-shirt under my one strap, that was another one of my favs. This was because my best friend Keira had bought it for me, a Fraggle Rock one, and I swear I nearly cried when she gave it to me, I was so happy. But then it was one of the many favourites of mine, being that the 80's was, in my opinion, the best era yet! But then why not, when it's about creatures that have a thirty minute working week, have fur tipped tails and seek wisdom from the 'all knowing, all seeing' Trash Heap, named Marjory, who was located in a corner of the Gorgs' garden. *Epic* story telling that, especially with the combined genius of the Doozers that basically looked cute in their mini hard hats and work boots. Oh, and they also built stuff for no real reason, only to have the Fraggles eat it, which would have pissed me off no end. As for my hair style now, it was currently in Princess Leia rolls with curls sticking out the centres, and I was killin' the style once again.

Right, well that's where we are on the whole mental image of me thing. Now, moving on to the where, why and who part. I currently live in a bitchin' pad known as Afterlife, and the best way to describe the place was a Gothic nightclub that had a baby with a castle. One that serves humans by night, and hides a hidden world of the supernatural up in the VIP and through the doors beyond. All of which was ruled and owned by the broody, bad ass King man who lives here.

A King who ran his hidden kingdom from the VIP area we got to spend most nights in, being that my husband and I worked for him. Meaning that we sat at his council table and were included in all the important shit. It was a cool gig really, mainly because I got to do this with my home girl, Keira, AKA Toots. This was because she was his totally awesome and cool wife, the Queen. Oh, and just so happened to be my bestie, beastie friend who basically couldn't live without me in her life, which is a total ditto mucho grando feeling.

You see the story really began when this King of

Kings, named one hottie but ultra-scary, Dominic Draven, found his Chosen One… okay so, Electus if you wanna get all Latin, old technical and shit! Well, anyway, this chick was human, named Keira and very, very, very, very, long ass story short, I worked for some other dude named Lucius (King of Vampires). Someone who ordered me and my hubby Adam to kidnap her. Which we totally did. But then when she turned out to be totally coolio and stuff, we became friends and have remained so ever since. Plus, I think it was really good how she didn't hold a grudge on the whole kidnapping thing or anything.

So, after a load of end of the world shit, we fought together, and she got herself knocked up with the beautiful Little Bean. One who was currently looking up at me with those big blues, blinking like she was trying to get her three-year-old brain to compute why her crazy aunty was killing flies with a flip flop that had been renamed,

FLY KILLER 5000 in glitter glue.

Not that there had been 4999 attempts or models before it, but I just thought 5000 sounded good. Plus, I thought 10000 was too showy. Now, I could go way, way, waaaay in depth with the story of Keira's life and the whole bunch of grape filled crazy juice, but well… haven't we done that already?

So, this time, it's my turn and my story to tell, something that started with the FLY KILLER 5000 and those big blue eyes… oh and the angry roar that shook the walls… yeah, better not forget that part, 'cause that's kinda important.

"Wha wis that, Aunty Pip?" the kid asked, one who has a name of course, but we will get to that in a bit. But first, that almighty roar, that ended in…

"Oh no, Pip, what did you do to him this time?" Toots asked, to which I answered…

"I might have been bad."

TWO

NERDY SNOOKEMS IS ANGRY

After Toots asked this, I winced.

Toots was my nickname for Keira, my bestie. Someone who was currently walking through into the sitting room with a cup of tea in hand, looking at the hallway with worry etched into her features. Of course, finding me balancing on the pyramid of antique furniture I had made didn't faze her in the slightest as, once again, she was used to me by now. Plus, we'd been through a war together, so shit like that was a great team building exercise in my opinion. Oh, and I am not even going to get into the whole time travelling Persian circus thing, as that's a whole 'Back to the Future' movie in itself!

Now, back to Toots, who looked perfect as she stepped into the regal looking sitting room that reminded me of a royal palace. She was blonde, gorgeous, blue eyed and was unfortunately taller than me, but not by much, being as she was five foot three. She also wore a black pencil skirt, with a white wraparound shirt that was tucked tight around her waist, with a big silk bow at her side. Basically, she was dressed like a sexy minx, and I totally knew why. See she worked with her husband dealing with the human side of business, and I knew first-hand the kick she got out of teasing her husband. We were similar like that as, well… where do you think she learned these skills from? And clearly, Mr Kingy Man Broody Pants had a thing for the whole sexy secretary getup.

But as for right now, she was clearly taking a tea break from teasing and work stuff to spend time with her Little Bean, who I was currently doing a shitty job of babysitting. But then, maybe fly killing missions and teaching her how to take her life into her own hands all in the name of insect destruction, was in the little person care book. Because in my defence, the fly had been bugging her by landing on her during our fort cushion building.

As for what Toots was referring to now, well that was what I had done to my husband, who I… erm… well, should we say, I tested a lot. But then, I was addicted to the punishments he would give me, so what can I say, sometimes I would have to get inventive. Because I swear, the guy was getting harder and harder to piss off with each passing century.

"Only what he deserves after breaking the head off my Battle Cat with his big feet, so now his armour doesn't fit properly, even after I glued the little… erm… buggie," I said, stopping myself from saying a bad word in front of a toddler. Although, it was like I said to Keira, I don't know why, as who did she think was going to be the one to teach her all the best curse words when she hit the age mummy thinks is cool? Like I said, she will need them, as kindergarten can be brutal. Only the other day, Little Bean came back with her favourite red crayon snapped in half… the bastards!

It was a brutal world.

Of course, her parents didn't really name her Little Bean, no, that one was all me, and about a hundred other nicknames as well… that was kinda my thing. No, her name was Amelia Faith Draven, Fae for short by her mum, but not mom because she was English and that's how they said it over there, giving umpf to the U like 'Bum'. Of course, when I pointed out this similarity, she hadn't looked impressed. But then I guess no one really appreciated being referred to as an ass, so I got it and took no offence.

"Oh no, not a buggie," Little Bean shouted in horror, making me smile down at her.

"I know, right." Then I winked at her, making the painted glitter stars over my eyes twinkle, causing Little Bean to giggle as I knew it would. But then the rumbling roar of anger started to get louder, as Adam had obviously managed to free himself from the chains I'd used... damn it, they were the strongest ones I could get and took me ages to find in Hell. I swear, his beast was getting stronger. Well, as long as my skinny ass could control him when he changed, then all was good and safe with the world.

"So, what was it this time, huh?" Toots asked, making me wink at her next, before suddenly my hubby in question burst into the room with his clothes ripped and near shredded. Oh dear, I came close to a partial shift this time... eeek.

Not. Good.

Suddenly, I shrieked out as my dungaree straps were

gripped in a tight fist and I was physically lifted off my unsteady mound of furniture. Then I was placed on my monster feet and soon found myself looking up at the very handsome, yet furious, face of Adam.

I swear I never got used to how gorgeous and yummy he was! I mean boy oh boy, I had lucked out in the husband department, it had to be said. Because not only was he utterly delicious to look at, he was also the kindest, sexiest, sweetest, most lovely and thoughtful person I knew. Plus, he almost always put up with my crazy antics, but major emphasis on the 'almost' in that sentence, as it was clear I was facing one of those rare 'almost moments'.

Of course, this angry face didn't take away from his beauty, it just gave him that raw edge he never normally displayed often. In truth, most people would look at my husband and think he was the least threatening one in the room. But then everyone knew that looks could be deceiving and, in this case, they most definitely were as, like I said, he was the most dangerous creature in existence.

But then, having a vessel that many thought looked like some kind of sexy accountant or professor was why many didn't find him a threat worth worrying over. Of course, they would have been wrong and in a 'oh shit, here comes the hulk' kinda way.

His usually well-kept appearance was long gone, and those thick black rimmed glasses he usually wore were crooked in his hurry to put them on. In truth, he didn't need them. He merely wore them out of habit, something he never could get out of since being human… like a comfort blanket.

A comfort blanket that sat upon a straight nose that matched the angular face of a male model. High cheekbones, defined chin and perfectly shaped lips, which currently were framed by a few days of stubble that made him look more rugged. Now, as for what he usually wore, well, he had that sexy Indiana Jones' professor look going on, making me paint a few words over my own eyelids a few times just to make him blush.

As for his fine male physic, he was tall and slim, but hid a body full of sexy lickable muscles behind layers of tweed and cotton… I'm talking six pack abs, defined biceps that had no trouble tossing my body around during sex, and corded forearms that just made me want to drool. Pecs that were muscled enough that they held pancake syrup in between the slight valley of flesh long enough for me to lick off, but not too much that he was a few pushed weights short of a man bra.

Oh, but the best part, his ass… that I swear made me want to live on all fours just so I could be closer to it. Not forgetting a pair of strong hands that drove me insane when they were kneading my flesh like he was some kind of baker God in a previous life!

"Erm, hi Nerdy Snookems," I said, in what I hoped was a cute enough way that he would calm down because I had to say, I was usually over his shoulder by now and heading my way to our bedroom for him to 'punish me'. Which meant I was getting concerned, as the whole staring angrily down at me thing was new, and something that admittedly had me a little worried.

"Oh no, don't you Nerdy Snookems me, you are not getting out of it this time by being cute, Winifred." I should also mention that Adam was the only one who ever called me this, unless a person was saying it in anger. Which right now, he was doing both.

"So, you admit that I am being cute?" I asked, trying to steer the conversation back into my favour… needless to say, it didn't work.

"No, no way… you are not doing that either!" he snapped, again something Adam rarely did, meaning I was really in trouble this time. This was when Keira got a hint that something wasn't right and picked up Little Bean and said,

"Come on, Fae bear, let's go get you one of the cookies we baked from the kitchen whilst Aunty Pip says sorry to Uncle Adam." Then she gave me a look and a nod behind his back, encouraging me to do just that. Something I was starting to think might be wise, as I didn't think a forgiving blow job was going to cut it this time… damn it, and I was so good at those.

"Can we see daddy?" I heard her sweet little voice ask her momma bear, and Toots laughed before her answer was heard as they walked down the hallway outside the open door,

"Sure thing, but only if you promise to get your sticky hands all over your daddy's new suit."

"And spwinklus!" she shouted in excitement, again making her mum laugh. But then all humour fled the room right along with them, leaving me staring up at a pair of angry hazel eyes that turned to caramel when he was turned on… something he most definitely freaking absolutely wasn't right now.

That's when it was confirmed…

I had gone too far.

I knew that two seconds after I said,

"Oh come on, Pookie, it was only a joke." This was when he growled low and started to back me up against the wall. Then he leaned closer to my face and slapped a piece of paper to the wall near my head, and snapped,

"Not. Fucking. Funny. Winifred." I turned my head and looked to see my fake 'your wife has been kidnapped' note I had created by cutting out different letters from magazines like they used to do in the movies… I wonder why they never did that anymore?

"Okay, so I might have gone too far this time," I admitted, making him give me an incredulous look before snapping,

"You think!" I then shrugged my shoulders and said in an unsure tone,

"I'm sorry?" Now this was said this way not because I wasn't sure if I was sorry or not, as I most definitely was, but more in a way I was unsure whether he would believe me or not, or if he would even want to hear that right now. He snarled before pushing away from the wall and turning his back to me. Then he crushed the note in his fist and heaved out a great sigh.

"Aww, baby… I really am sorry… I was just… or maybe I didn't… erm… think," I said, feeling myself getting upset. Damn it, I hated hurting him and that in turn hurt me. Gods, I was such an idiot! I knew that when he started shaking his head.

"I don't understand you, Winnie… why, why would you try and push me so hard?"

"You know why, baby," I said softly, making him bark,

"As hard as this?!" he said, throwing the note to the floor before taking one look down at it, his eyes heating enough for it to ignite instantly from his glare. I swallowed hard before pulling the ball of my lip piercing into the side of my mouth, a nervous gesture I rarely showed. His eyes homed in on it, knowing what it was and making him release a deep sigh of frustration.

"I nearly turned fully, Winnie," he told me, making me nod in understanding before telling him,

"But you didn't."

"And what do you think would have happened if I had turned… did you think about that!?" he barked back, making me wince as I hated it when he shouted at me, even despite knowing that I deserved it right now. Because the truth was, Adam rarely ever shouted at me which meant that when he did, I could never handle it. Of course, I also knew that when I wiped away my tears with the back of my hand, he would hate seeing it too.

"But yyy…ou did…n't," I hiccupped out. He tensed as if fighting with himself on what he wanted to do and what he thought he had to do.

"I could have ripped this place apart… I could have destroyed this whole fucking place and hurt… damn it, Pip, I could have hurt Amelia!" he shouted, as if the very thought brought him even greater pain and he was right, it was foolish.

"I didn't… I didn't think."

"That's right! You didn't think and that's the problem, Winnie, you never fucking think!" he shouted back, making me flinch as if he had struck me by his own hand… something he would never do. But then the second he saw the pain he had inflicted by his words, he let out another sigh, and this one had his own regret written all over it.

"Winnie, I shouldn't have…"

"No. You're right… you're right as always, Adam… I…I think you should just… I should just…" I stopped then and burst into tears before running from the room, hearing only one thing as I did.

A whisper from the only man I'd ever loved…

"Oh, Turtle Dove."

THREE

GUILTY IMP

I ran.

I ran and Adam didn't follow.

That was huge. No, that was planet sized colossal, because Adam always came after me. He hated seeing me upset and always tried to dry my tears. Not that I cried for that reason. Come on, I was a crazy handful, but I wasn't a manipulative bitch. In fact, I hated getting upset in front of people. I hated making people feel uncomfortable around me and well, a never ending stream of tears running down my face usually did that. So I always tried to cry alone. Of course, Adam was always usually there, even if I tried to hide away. Because he was my comfort blanket. He was my saviour, my protector, and my knight in demonic skin and a nerdy vessel combined.

Adam was my everything.

Of course, after being together since the 1600's, I couldn't exactly claim this as the first time I had pissed him off… I mean, this was still me we were talking about here. But no matter how much I had messed up in the past, he had never let me cry alone…

Not once.

Not in over four hundred years.

"Gods, just how much can you screw up, Winifred?" I asked myself, before I let my hands catch my head as I cried into my palms. Then I shuddered and let out a stream of hiccups that came out when I tried to breathe through my pain and guilt.

I was a fool.

But the truth was, I had to keep pushing him.

It had been my only warning of what would happen if I didn't.

In the end I don't know how long I stayed out on that rooftop, sat staring out at the rolling green mountains. Mountains that seemed to go on forever and if an alien come to this planet and landed right here not knowing any better, they could think these mountains covered the Earth they were so big. Man, but I kinda wished some Scotty would have beamed me up just then and to save the world they needed my help. But in doing so, had to turn back time so I could tell my younger self not to make that stupid note!

Damn you Star Trek for not being real!

I don't know how long I was out there feeling sorry for myself but by the time I went back to the sitting room, it had been long enough for momma bear and baby bear to be back.

"Here, Wanty Pip, I brought you back a cookie with extra prinkles... I mean spinkles," Little Bean said, making my broken heart melt back together.

"Thanks, mini bestie," I said, putting a smile on my face which was basically like my armour. Then Toots came up to me and gave me a hug before framing my face with her hands and using her thumbs to wipe away my streaky make up.

"You okay, honey?" she asked, making me swallow down the emotion and nod as my throat didn't want to work to create words.

"I saw him, he wanted me to make sure you're okay," Toots told me, making my heart soar before saying,

"He did?!"

"Yeah, he did," she replied grinning. After this I rammed in my cookie and said with a mouthful,

"I etter go find himmm." But then I only got as far as the door before Toots said,

"Erh, Pip, I wouldn't do that." I frowned, and swallowed my now sugary cookie dough like it had turned to lead.

"Why not?" That was when my best friend started to look uncomfortable, before answering me,

"He also told me to tell you that he needed time… erm… *apart.*" I closed my eyes as a shuddered breath ripped through me at the pain that one word brought me…

Apart.

As in not together. As in separate… as in… *alone.*

Toots could see me about to crumble into a sticky Pip shaped mess on the floor, and quickly ran over to me and took me in her arms before whispering to me,

"It doesn't mean that, so don't even think it, honey. He's just mad, that's all." I nodded on her shoulder as she patted my back.

"Trust me, Draven could make brooding an Olympic

sport when we fight about something… but they always come around," she told me when I pulled back and wiped my tears to hide them from Little Bean.

"Wah is broo die mean?" her daughter asked, making me grin and say,

"Good luck with that one." Then I winked at Toots when she groaned,

"Yeah, well it's going to be easier than explaining 'man meat stick', so thanks for that." I laughed before saying,

"Ooops, my bad." Keira laughed and said,

"Yeah, well you're not the one who had to explain to your husband why his daughter was eating a kebab and asking for another man meat stick… Jesus, but I thought Draven was going to have a heart attack!" At this I burst out laughing and in truth, Toots always had that ability to make me laugh, even during times like this. But then, she was awesome and my best friend for a reason.

"So come on, Pip, what did you do this time?" she asked after we had sat down and she had her daughter bouncing on her knee, after explaining 'broody' was another word for a man paddy. But this question also came with a wrinkled nose, that had I not been so sad about being in the mucho dog house, I would've passed comment about looking cute to Toots. But, unfortunately for me, I'd pissed Adam off and clearly hit a new limit when doing so, which I wasn't sure that I could blame him for as now I'd thought about it, it was a shitty thing I had done.

"Okay, I confess I might, maybe, slightly, not completely, but most probably, undecidedly…"

"Pip, seriously, before I start showing wrinkles, and I'm immortal, so you get the point…"

"Okay, fine. I might have written a letter like a kidnapper's ransom note saying I had been kidnapped and left it stuck to his head with potentially a little bit of glue that might or might not have been of the super variety," I said, wincing, as it did actually sound worse than what I had originally intended. Of course, the moment that Toots started to rub her forehead in the way that most people do when they think I've fucked up, I understood it was a hell of a lot worse than what I first assumed it would be.

"Oh Pip, I love you, but I really don't understand what goes through your mind sometimes when you do these things," she said with a groan, and even little three nearly four year old Amelia slapped her hand to her forehead, shook her head, and said,

"Not good, Wanty Pip." Which meant that intelligence

wise, I had been out-beaten by a toddler, for even she knew that what I had done had been wrong.

"Alright, so yes, mucho on the stupid but in my defence…" I paused to let Toots groan before continuing,

"I have to keep pushing him."

"But why? I mean, we have known each other for quite some time now, and yet I still don't understand why you continue to push his limits knowing what he could… you know…" Keira said, rolling her hand around as if not wanting to talk about Adam's beast in front of her little girl. But then again, Amelia was no normal little girl, despite being born mortal. But mortal or not, she was as intuitive as they came, smart as a button… although how buttons got labelled with the smart card I have no idea, but then again, I had no idea how they got labelled with the cute card either… I was starting to think there was something secretive about buttons as they were both cute and smart. Okay, squirrel moment over, you get my point, the girl was well above the pay grade, age card in intelligence. At this rate she would end up being like some sexy, beautiful Rain man, Marie Curie, Hawkins, Albert Einstein, and Gladys West combined! Basically, she was one smart cookie, who right now smelled like a cookie and had half of it around her face. But then momma bear whipped out a baby wipe from nowhere, which I swear since having a kid had become one of her superpowers!

I swear wipes had invaded Afterlife, as I found one in my shoe one day and spent half the night wondering why Mr Lefty was feeling damp... and yes, my feet were male.

But getting off my feet and their baby wipe troubles, I released a sigh and replied to her question.

"But that's exactly why I have to keep pushing him, because the more I do it, the stronger he gets fighting against it. It's a bit like yoga."

"Yeah, you're gonna have to explain that one to me," Toots said, after tucking her long blonde hair behind her ear and leaning forward to let Little Bean slide off her knee so she could go back to playing in our cushion fort.

"You know, the more you do yoga, the stretchier you get, more bendy and what not, like a pretzel. But then you stop doing yoga for a bit and you become a breadstick, one that's already baked and therefore can no longer become pretzel... you get me, downward dog achiever?" I said, making Amelia giggle from inside the tent of sofa squares I had used to make the bulk of the structure. As for Toots, well she just squinted her eyes a little bit and tilted her head to one side, which was a clear indication that she was really trying to get it but the metaphor was a little bit lost on her, and now… well… most likely we both wanted a pretzel because, hello, pretzels are way better than bread sticks and kick their skinny asses.

"I see you're struggling with this, so in a nutshell, here it is… if Adam stopped having things happen that pushed him to the limit, then he wouldn't be able to control himself when the small things happened. He would get complacent and in those moments that say, his tea bag split or he got punched in the face, because despite what the Joker says in the original Batman movie, people do hit other people with glasses, then he wouldn't be able to control himself," I said, thinking I had made myself quite clear, yet she continued to rub her forehead like well, like her husband often does when he is too confused around me. This now made me wonder if they actually had been rubbing off on each other in these last six years.

"Okay, so I think I understand what you're saying."

"You do?" I asked in a hopeful tone.

"Yeah, you push him so that he can control himself better." I was just about to shout bingo wings when Amelia spoke first,

"I think you got it, mummy," she said, looking up at her mother as if she was her whole world, and I had to say it definitely pulled on my mummy heartstrings myself, seeing as I would have wanted nothing more than to have children. But that's where things got complicated in my world, see that nutshell I was talking about... that was pretty much how I was born...

Yep, I was literally a NUT.

FOUR

AN IMP IS BORN

Yes, that's right, you heard me correctly…

A Nut.

You see, Imps didn't come from Hell and they didn't come from Heaven. No, we came from a Realm that was between the two. I'm a Shadow Imp which means that I was created on the darker side of the Mother Tree, the side closer to Hell, which meant that many classed us as demons for that reason.

But I know what you're thinking, what in holy nut world was the Mother Tree?

Well now, the Mother Tree was a whole new

conversation in itself. But, running along the same nut theme we're going with, then in that same nutshell is a lot of otherworldly creatures which would have been classed as mythology in the mortal world, that were born from that same Mother Tree. And once again, I know what you're thinking, *is there like a tree for everything in this world?* And yeah, you're pretty much right with that. There was the Tree of Life, the Tree of Souls (which may or may not be connected to Lucius, depending on which side of mythology you believed in). There was the Tree of Death, the Tree of Darkness and Nightmares, along with many others I can't be bothered to list. But basically, every bugger in a Realm had a Tree they called their own, and one every Tom, Dick and Van Dyke was connected to in some way. But for me, well, there was the Mother Tree.

Now this Mother Tree connected all of the Fae Realms, and depending on which side of the Tree you were born from, depended on what you would become. Imps, like myself, were actually more like chestnuts, making me, what I like to consider, one of the Conkers of the Supernatural world.

Cool, huh?

Now, like I said, dependant on which side of the Realm

we were born on, we would fall to the Earth and then grow into what destiny or some other malarky, hocus pocus chose for us.

Which was why you had lots of different types of Imps; Shadow Imps like me, who like I said, were born on the Hellish side of the Tree closer to Hell. But you also have Forest Imps, Water Imps, Imps of the Lost, which were born naturally in the Lost Lands, just to name a few. But then, it wasn't only Imps that were born from its branches.

It was said that the tree gained its powers from the Eternal Fountain which was rumoured to be protected deep underground in its own Temple... jeez, but where there was a special Tree, there was bound to be a Temple. But the Trees' roots relied on this Fountain of the Gods that was said to grant life in the Elemental Realms.

Now, as for the creatures that dominated these lands, they were of course those pointy eared dickheads, the arrogant Fae. Or, if you want to use their fancy pants name, the Elves. Although, they didn't really like the term Elves much, hence why I enjoyed using it. This was because, to them, the Imps were classed as lower beings, which just poked at my goat... and well, let's just say my goat liked to bite!

Okay, so I didn't exactly have a goat... well, not anymore... poor Jeffery... but come on, lower class... ha, well considering I ended up being destined for one of the most powerful beings on Earth, take that Fakings! Naturally, I called them this because they were Fae Kings... get it, *fakings*... anyway, I didn't like the bastards, so that was that.

But getting back to me, well, I was a little different... and not just in the quirky sense. Because it was true, I was a nut that had been created on the shadow side, but after I had fallen to the Earth, that was when things had got tricky. You see, even before I took root underground, I was a mischievous little sort. I split from my shell and rolled away from where I should have landed. Because, in truth, Shadow Imps were usually a lot darker, a lot more with the sinister side should we say. Basically, they were bitches and bastards and every mean thing in between.

However, I hadn't been like that, which meant I had been an outcast the moment I had sprouted up from the Earth and tried to make my way back to where I knew I would find my dark home.

Needless to say, I wasn't exactly welcomed with open arms, so I left and after a cruel journey to Hell, I heard about the Mortal Realm and discovered that people were nice there. Oh, of course there could be cruelty in the Mortal Realm, what with human nature and what not, but it was the first time that I'd felt accepted, so this Conker stayed.

"That's all great, Pip, but I don't know how we got onto the topic of you being born," Keira said, making me realise that I had been speaking out loud and thankfully, because Little Bean was here, I had kept it rated appropriately with my language... ish, although I cursed like a sailor in my mind.

I was just about to open my mouth when suddenly Toots' phone started to ring.

"Hey, honey," she answered, telling me who was on the other end of the phone, her hubby, the mighty King of Kings, Dominic Draven. Mr dark, tall, hot and like I said... broody. Although, he had it totally bad for his own little mortal, who was now so much more.

When they first met, she had been a waitress working at his club, which meant that after it was discovered she was his Chosen Fated One, well, then the King decided to take what was owed to him by the Gods themselves. Of course, not everything bent easily to this Man Plan of his, because hello, women had strong opinions about shit like kidnapping. And well, being one of Keira's kidnappers (which trust me, there had been enough to start a club) then trust me again, I had the authority to comment on this subject.

"I want to speak to daddy!" little Amelia shouted in excitement, and Toots, being the best mum in the world, picked up her daughter and put her on her knee before putting the phone to her daughter's ear.

"Daddy, Daddy, Daddy, Daddy!" she started to sing, and I could hear his booming laughter on the other end. Watching the three of them together as a close knit family tugged at my little Imp heart, that was for sure. I loved them so much and was privileged to be included in their little trifecta, but as I thought back on my life and where it all began, I couldn't help but wonder at the choices I had made that had led to this point. I didn't know whether it was because I had argued with Adam, my poopy pants and keeper of my heart, but I felt the need to reflect on my decisions.

In fact, I was so deep in my zone, I didn't realise that the phone call had ended, and Toots was once again speaking to me.

"I have to go and help with this meeting... do you mind looking after her a little while longer?" The biggest grin took over my face because other than spending time with my husband and my best friend, then spending time with Little Bean was my favourite thing to do.

"Sure thing, in fact, I was thinking about writing a sorry note, so maybe you can help me write it and we could decorate it... what do you think? I think if we both put our heads together, we can't go wrong," I said, making her giggle before running back over to me, putting a hand out ready for our secret handshake, telling me,

"Let's do this!" I grinned, slapped my palm to hers, although somewhat more gently than I would an adult, and after a series of finger wagging hand shaking, elbow bumping, and palm spitting, we completed our secret handshake.

"Thanks, Pip, you're a star and don't worry about Adam, you know he always forgives you. But maybe you wanna tone it down on the crazy antics just to give him a rest. And remember, tomorrow is always a new day." I pounded the side of my fist to my chest and gave her a salute, telling her,

"Right on, sister!" After that, she left me and her

daughter to our own devices, which included me telling her,

"Right, it's time to pick some paint."

"Paint? I thought we were writing the letter?" she asked, cocking her head to the side and making her pigtails tip. I knelt down to her height, and tugged her little T-shirt that said,

'DEAR MONDAY,
GO STEP ON LEGO'

One that I bought her, naturally. This awesome T-shirt had been combined with little jeans that had rainbows on the pockets and unicorn patches on the knees. Little mini skull converse completed the look that was a gift to my bestie, as she had the same adult pair.

"Yeah, we are, but we're doing it Pip style." At this, her eyes grew wide, and she opened her mouth and said,

"Oh, dear." Then I winked at her and stood, before taking her adorable little hand and leading her out of the sitting room, leaving behind my FlyKiller 5000.

So, as we walked the hallways of Afterlife, we swung our arms like we always did and made our way to the righteous part of this cool Gothic popsicle stand, that was where me and my Pookie lived. Needless to say, once Amelia had discovered her legs were for walking, then it had been advised that I keep a lock on the apartment that me and Adam lived in. Of course, I knew why, me and my husband were known somewhat as a very sexual couple. Basically, we did it like BDSM bunnies, which meant that many things in our room were not exactly of the appropriate kind for a little curious mind. Which also meant, that no one wanted a three year old getting hold of their vibrating dildo and asking exactly what it was… not even me. Someone who would have probably had about twenty answers to that, one of which would have been a rotating tower for when your building blocks made a castle.

But, knowing that the Tooternator would have probably freaked out and given her gorgeous self a substantial hernia, I decided to have a feng shui moment and change our living space to be more suitable for the Little Bean. because let's face it, of course I wanted her to come and play in my room. That was the best thing about kids, their playful side! And considering I had an imagination that had often been referred to as childlike, there was a reason that Amelia called me her favourite auntie, or should I say, Wanty.

Now, I couldn't claim to be her only aunty, as she had two other aunts. Amelia also adored her mortal Aunty Libby, who was of course Keira's sister. I liked her too, as she was fun and always laughed at my jokes. Which was a major what I liked to call a monusblus with me... translation, *bonus plus*

Then there was Sophia, another one of my besties. Someone who was again her actual Aunt by blood, being that she was the sister of Dominic Draven. But the downside to Sophia was that she was a bit of a germaphobe and also lived for fashion. Unfortunately, that also meant that for a toddler like Little Bean who pretty much was a giant germ with legs and had no interest in fashion whatsoever, the only thing they really shared together was when it came to dressing her dolls.

Not that this was an 'aunty competition' or anything, but let's just say that Sophia wasn't exactly ready to go jumping in muddy puddles dressed as a pig, and I'm not talking of the 'Peppa' variety. I mean, if you're gonna do it dressed like a pig, then do it right. However, Sophia did excel in the tea party department, and this too was something they enjoyed immensely together, especially when Sophia encouraged her to put pretty pink bows in her husband Zagan's hair... something the demon had no problem with, because this was Little Bean we were talking about. Everyone, and I mean *everyone*, loved Little Bean. Which also meant that she had the most powerful beings on Earth wrapped around her cute little fingers. This included the big bad ass men who lived at Afterlife. So yes, it was also known that Dominic Draven himself would end up taking council meetings with his daughter bouncing on his lap and sticking lollypops in his face or trying to plait his hair.

Vincent, his brother, would often laugh at his expense which always ended the same way, with Dom telling his daughter that it was her uncle's turn to get a ribbon. To which she would never be denied as Vincent, the King of Angels, adored his niece and became a slave to anything she wanted... bow and ribbons and sticky candy included.

Now, as for me, well like I said, I was somewhat classed as a favourite as everyone knew that when it came to fun, Pip was the one you called. Hence the reason why, when entering my private space, above the door was written in lights...

PIP AND ADAM'S FUNHOUSE.

Well, it certainly lived up to that name, and naturally was one of Little Bean's favourite places to spend her time. Of course, this could be down to a number of reasons. Perhaps it was the adventure wall we had built, that was complete with half a pirate ship and a plank you could walk that jumped into a pile of cushions shaped like sharks and waves.

But then it could have also been the sofa which sat in the centre of the room that was like the basket on a hot air balloon. One that was actually attached to a rainbow balloon above hanging from the ceiling, and one that you had to climb up a rope ladder to get into. But this wasn't all, as there were slides that landed into a ball pit, seating that was a patchwork of colours that were written on like pages from story books. There was a sweet shop decorated like the land of Willy Wonka, and complete with an animatronic Oompa Loompa that stood behind the counter asking what you wanted.

As for our bed, it was a giant nest filled with egg-shaped cushions and a hamburger sofa, that you squeezed in between and could snuggle up between buns with a blanket of cheese, tomato, and lettuce.

Of course, Adam and I reserved our, lets call it naughty side, for behind locked doors and had a secret room built. Which meant I was quite used to hearing things like, why don't you have a cool room like Aunty Pip and Uncle Adam, Mum and Dad? Of course, a naughty wink directed at Toots and her husband was too much of an opportunity to miss, seeing as they knew what we had built behind a secret door.

But I was lucky, I had great people in my life and the family I had always dreamed of. But it wasn't always like this, there had once been a time I was alone, and I had been sad. I thought about what my life was like before I met Adam; before I met my beast.

I quickly found I had to stop and squash down the tears that threatened when thinking about all the wonderful things I could lose should Adam really walk away.

But then, as if Amelia could sense where my mind was at, she asked me a question that felt like the very start of where my long life really started being lived...

"Wanty Pip... *how did you meet Uncle Adam?*"

STEPHANIE HUDSON

FIVE

A PIPER'S PLAN FOR A PIP
22ND MARCH 1603

O nce again, I tugged at the uncomfortable embroidered doublet with its epaulettes and short tab skirt. I looked down with vexatious disdain at the gathered breaches, matching canions, blue hose and high heeled shoes with their large rosettes. Gods, but a gentleman's clothes were all near as uncomfortable as what was considered fashionable for ladies these days. In short, anything you encased your body in of this era was uncomfortable, no matter what you wore. It made me long for a hotter country, and one where I could get away with wearing very little due to the heat.

Such as a toga, upon my wordsmith, I missed wearing togas.

But for me togas were, unfortunately, a thing of the past as here I was, currently dressed like a gentleman because it was safer that way when travelling on a ship unaccompanied by a husband or without a chaperone. However, I believed that word 'fashion' had to be used in the loosest sense, especially for men, for they looked anything but manly. Now, as for the Irishman, then I believed they had it right, with their knee length capes and tunics with high standing collars and checked woollen hose, for at least they looked a damn sight more attractive than the English gentleman, especially as they didn't have silly roses stuck to their feet!

Alas, in truth I preferred men to look like men, but then I had spent more time in a man's company before the use of a curly wig. Take the Trojan warriors for example, now those boys knew how to dress, I thought with a wicked smile. But then again, I also remembered swooning after quite a few knights had swung their swords on the battlefield, which was a double entendre if ever there was one.

But I also loved it when they came back dirty and in need of a good washing... among other things... even if it took half the night to get them naked and get to the fun parts.

Of course, wearing this man's doublet wasn't exactly made any more comfortable over the tight boned corset I had forced my little paps into... although paps were a common name for breasts, I had to say I preferred the newer term of lily white balls, which in my body of circumstance, they most certainly were... *little... white... balls.*

Oh, to be free again and let my lilies out into the world. I felt that in every new era I lived through, I had to relearn new etiquette and ways to fit in. In truth, if I didn't enjoy my comforts, like sleeping on a bed and food that came in the form of being wrapped in pastry, then I probably would have become some wild woman of Borneo, living in the rainforest. Or maybe back to Persia, living the life of luxury in some old rich man's harem somewhere, and I could wear some scantily clad outfits that would shock and horrify the elite of London.

Gah, London, the smog of the earth, I could barely breathe in that cesspool, one I would soon be finding myself in once again. But I did not know why Pan had wanted to come back to London, and these days it was becoming more and more about what my lover wanted and it was all about keeping him happy. In truth, I was starting to wonder why I was still with him, and I was pretty sure he was not the best of choices for me. Besides, I had started to hear rumours, whispers, and tales of legend particularly from the town of Hamelin, Lower Saxony, Germany.

But then, rumours were most of the time just that. Tragic whispers that travelled the wind and blew the sails of ships that sailed the oceans from one continent to the other. It was exciting times, especially after Italian explorer Christopher Columbus had led four Spanish transatlantic expeditions to the Americas. There was even talk of the first real colony being established there, yet when such a thing was to come to fruition was anyone's guess. However, I didn't believe they would be short of volunteers, as many people were desperate to escape religious persecution and the New World was rumoured to offer such reprieve.

Of course, there had been many failures before this year, but then I often believed that it was through a person's mistakes that the most important lessons were learned… I was wise in that way. Now, all I needed to do was take this practice of words upon my own standing, as I was starting to believe that Pan was one mistake it may be too late to learn from.

Take this latest task he had thrust upon me, and the reason I was currently dressed like a gentleman travelling alone. This was because there were still some sailors that believed the presence of women would anger the water gods, which in truth, was just laughable really. Especially when the likes of Poseidon and Pontus were some of the randiest bastards of the sea. They would have loved having more woman challenging their oceans on a journey, for they were often breaking the rules and taking liberties with a mortal girl.

Of course, the most obvious reason not to have a woman aboard was down to the lusts of mortal men and their own sexual appetites. So, as it was frowned upon for women travelling, and Pan was definitely not about to volunteer me as being his wife, he instead recommended I dress like a gentleman. Or should I say 'boy' as better use of the word, for I was short of stature and slim to the point of being classed as underfed, something I would no doubt have died from had I not been immortal, for I did indeed find myself without food on many a belly grumbling occasion. This was because I would not steal from those less fortunate, no matter how hungry I was. Because mortals had it far worse and my vessel could last, whereas theirs could not.

Also, another indication of Pan not being right for me was that he encouraged me to stay underfed and kept me skinny, for this then meant I could easily fit into small spaces when it came to stealing the things that *he* wanted. An immoral act I would only carry out if the taking was from the rich and those who could afford to lose something.

But, like I said, Pan was not the best male companion a girl could have, I was starting to see that now, and this long journey had given me time enough to open my eyes to that fact. No matter how good it felt to make the beast with two backs. Fucking, basically.

However, as a Shadow Imp born on the wrong side of the shadows, and essentially where the sun shone, I found myself with little choices in life. It was mistake after mistake I grant you, and it was now the reason that I looked at myself in the mirror and released a sigh of frustration. This, before tucking my ruby red curls back up into this ridiculous tall hat with its thick band and wide brim. So, I ran my fingertips along the rim, nodded to myself and said,

"Time to be bad." Then I cleared my throat and deepened my usual singsong voice, knowing that I sounded more like I was imitating a pirate, that, or a farmer from Somerset. I had also used a wire brush on some dusting of coal to darken my chin and jawline to make it look like I had at least some sort of growth on my face. After all, I was trying to pass as a boy who had at least come in to some sort of manhood, and that my bollocks had dropped at least.

I closed my bright green and blue eyes, that mimicked the colour of the grass I had been born and emerged from like all Imps do from the ground. Then I tugged down at my doublet one more time before I made my way out of the quarters of the ship. Naturally, Pan hadn't taken this journey with me, but then again, he never did. No, he was too much of a wanted man worldwide, and I wondered when it would be that England would also class him as such. I also wondered which corner of the world he would try next, for there wasn't yet enough to steal in the New World.

Well, this would be the last time I joined him, no matter how much I enjoyed shaking the sheets with him. At the very least, he had said that he would meet me in London, as after all... I had a special cargo to deliver. Yet it was odd, for I hadn't known that Pan had been particularly fond of rats, yet he believed they would help our new life together greatly. He had told me that this would be his last job and these rats would represent that, for he knew how fond I was of owning pets. And he believed these would be perfect, as he told me that rats from China were lucky.

Now, I knew I was known to be somewhat naïve, but even I suspected there was more to this than what I had allowed myself to believe. Because even I knew that they were called vermin for a reason, although I felt that was somewhat unfair and unjust. I mean, they were just another living creature trying to survive any way they could. I suppose, in truth, I sympathised with the poor little mites, for I too was terribly misunderstood. And it was strange, for I truly felt like there hadn't yet been a society or an era that I had really fitted into. It was as though I was still waiting for history to catch up with me and I just needed to keep living this grey, colourless life until finally reaching a future filled with a rainbow of better things.

Because everything seemed so bleak, so macabre. And this no more so than in the cities where people literally lay in the streets and slept with their own faeces. The slums of the city were like a diseased body rotting at its core and spreading outwards. But then, even in the best of places, people still needed the use of a snuff box to make it home without vomiting because of the stench.

Quite honestly, London was far behind its times, for even the city of Mohenjo-Daro from the early bronze age had clean wells, water pipes and had invented a better way of disposing of their own shit. For water was life, and when you lived in a city where drinking ale was better for your health than the polluted water supply, then even for a ditsy (my own word) Imp, there was clearly a problem. But the 'Standard', near the junction of Cornhill and Leadenhall Street, had been the first mechanically pumped public water supply in London. It had been erected (which just so happened to be one of my most favoured words) in 1582, done so on the site of earlier hand-pumped wells and gravity-fed conduits. I mention this for it had been an idea I myself had implanted in the engineer's mind, for he had been responsible for solving the solution of water for London's people. Yet for reasons unknown to me, the service had been disconnected this year, according to Pan's letters.

But that was the nature of an Imp, we were known somewhat as the problem solvers of the supernatural world. Well, when we were taken seriously enough for those that believed themselves above us to listen. Those pointy eared fopdoodles, the bloody Elves, were just so damn superior to all others in the Elemental Realms, I was surprised they could wipe their own asses without tipping over due to their inflated ego heads!

Needless to say, I didn't much care for those magical blood sacks.

"Come on then, Percival, time to meet your new daddy," I said as I picked up my bag, one that contained a single rat that I had quickly declared as my favourite, hence why he travelled by my side. Unlike the others who travelled in my trunk that was filled with cages. I had allowed them to run around the cabin as much as possible, knowing that they would listen to me as my other skills as an Imp were being able to control the nature of some creatures. But as for Percival, well he was sticking with me.

I exited my quarters, lugging the heavy trunk behind me and struggled my way across the starboard side, saying things like,

'Out of my way, you scurvy dog, and shipper me timbers… which I think was said wrong, but then again, I'd been corrected quite a few times during this journey, so make of that what you will.

I crossed the plank over to the docks in Southampton, knowing I was then to get a carriage to London, despite it hardly being the season for it. Every time I found myself in the city, its population had grown having repopulated itself after the disastrous depletion in numbers, thanks to the horrific Black Death. A disease so deadly that when it hit in the 14th century it wiped out over half of the population, killing millions. Of course, no one knew what started the outbreak, only that it had swept across the world like a demonic force and annihilated human life in its path. To this day, no one really knew the exact numbers, we only remembered the piles of bodies that had to be buried and the smell of death that clung to the air thick enough to turn even a demon's stomach. Most immortals were quite impervious to those that were mortally inflicted as we didn't tend to mix.

But I had been affected.

Another lesson learned, and one that fractured my heart. Because never would I engage in mortal life that way again. No longer would I pretend to be one of them, even if the friendships I had made I could class as the greatest my life had known so far. But when the disease took them from me, no matter what I tried to do to help, I was helpless to stop it. That was when I learned why immortals didn't mix too deeply with those fated to die by the Gods.

But alas, that hadn't been the last time I had cried over the loss of mortal life, for the sights I had witnessed during such a time had made me long for the type of solitude only found in the untouched and unspoiled parts of the world. So, I had escaped it all after the day I was forced to watch my friends burn inside their infected homes, begging for a God I knew wouldn't save them.

It had made me question my life, and the answer was one only ever found for an Imp like me in nature. So, I had run from it all, escaping the last years of the Black Death until the world had been cleansed once again. That was when Pan had found me, fifty years later, playing his pipe and luring me from my cave, a place I had made my home. He had lured me from my grief and back into the world of mortals once more, with promises that he would protect me.

I had to confess, that for a while it had been good. The first hundred years or so we'd had fun and travelled all over Europe. But then, as each year passed, I felt my own soul darken, and that demonic side of me had awakened to a point of no return. Which meant that what I saw in the mirror these days wasn't the same Imp that had fled heartbreak that day.

Pan was the darkness that had been slowly blinding me.

I was sure of it.

As for Pan of the now, he had arranged a coach for me to get me to the city. It was said that the stagecoach was aiming to get an infrastructure put in place so that routes could become more frequent. This then making it easier for people to travel, but they were some years away from that, as with many things. It made me look up into the sky and wonder when mortals would invent wings.

The journey was to take a few days, and I had to say that the idea of being sat dressed as a man with a single rat as my companion didn't exactly fill me with joy. But then Pan was not exactly the type of person that you vexed, and I seemed to have an uncanny ability to be able to do it on a regular basis. To be honest, those questions of my future with him became more and more frequent, wondering if there was anyone out there for me?

But then I would remember the long hours of pleasure he could give me with his tongue, and stopped questioning it long enough to get in the carriage where my journey began yet again. Yet time was a funny thing to an immortal, as in some instances it seemed to go by in a blink of an eye and others it was painfully slow.

Like this journey, that gave me endless hours to reflect on life, yet again. On what I had gained and what I had lost.

But more than anything it made me wonder…

Who was I to…

Lose my heart to next?

SIX

BROKEN HEARTED DEATH
25ᵀᴴ MARCH 1603

China.

Now why in the dickens rats from China? I had questioned this for a while now and still did. Ever since following the silk roads all the way to the nearest port, where I caught the first merchant ship I could from Caffa before crossing the Black Sea. Then from there I made it to Constantinople, to Messina before bribing my way onto another ship to take me as far as Marseille. Once there, I once again found myself on a carriage, until the last ship of my journey could take me from Calais to the port of

Southampton. In short, my journey had been long enough to question, why the rats?

Pan had said they were lucky, these black rats from China known as the Rattus Rattus. Now these cousins to the larger brown rat were also known as little geniuses by my kind. Of course, this was because we could communicate with them on a basic level, and as such, there was a great deal to be learned from the smart little rodent. Now, rodent in itself came from the word, 'Rodere', which meant, 'To gnaw', and gnaw they most certainly could. They could eat their way through lead, concrete or even the sun-baked clay bricks of adobe.

They could also climb almost vertical walls and fit into spaces a quarter inch thick, making me wonder if Pan needed them for a job of some kind. Did he need them to fit into somewhere tiny and that was why he picked the little geniuses? I mean, these guys were that savvy that they would literally problem solve a situation, making a nest and creating an escape route just in case. They could also adapt to their environments at the drop of a capotain, not that I would drop one, for I had wanted to buy one of those hats for months now.

But back to these little darling black rats, and well,

they hadn't exactly been hard to find, for, let's just say that it would only take two rats making butter with one's tail, continuously for three years to lead to a population of over three million… granted that would be a lot of fucking and butter churning, which we all knew involved a lot of vigorous, circular movements, hence the saying. So, they were not exactly hard to locate.

Of course, I had questioned Pan on the reason for this mission, but his answer had been vague. Good pets and what not. Then he would swiftly speak of the next job, and one where he would be paid enough that we could finally settle. A payoff so large he said, that we could afford a nice big townhouse in the city. Although, when I had mentioned I'd much rather have one in the country, he scoffed at that.

To be honest, he scoffed at a lot of things I said.

But like I said, there had been much to think about during my time crossing the lands and oceans. In fact, by the time the journey finally came to its end, I admittedly was an exhausted little Imp. And as much as I was a fan of the furry smart guys, I was getting tired of heaving around the large trunk they were kept in. Not Percival though… never Percival.

Now this thinking had also led me to look back on what

usually happened when I questioned Pan too much on the shady decisions he made. And let's just say that the bastard had a brutal backhand, and the more years that went by the less patient he was with my questions.

Which was why I decided the next time he would do something like that, no matter how good he was with his tongue, I was kicking him back. Yes, and I would do so in such a way that his favourite appendage most likely wouldn't be classed as much use for filling holes for quite some time. Alas, my hope was that it would turn a rather angry shade of purple before swelling, and not in a good way, before eventually falling off.

Oh, indeed these last few days had given me a lot of cause for thought and after a deeper, more meaningful conversation with Percival, I decided that Pan was going to have to go. That I would aid him in what this last job of his may be, and then take my dues and find myself a new situation. Find myself a nice country estate to work at. A fine idea if ever I created one. It be true that my skills of baking bread weren't exactly up to par, but even I had to admit my needlework was to be envied by most.

By the Gods, I was finally going to make it on my own.

Yes, good plan, Pipper.

Of course, like most plans I made, it kind of fell to pieces the moment I arrived in London, where Pan met me and started manhandling me off the carriage. Pan, it couldn't be denied, was a handsome man. Which was unfortunate, as together with his talented tongue… it made him all the more harder to leave. But there was something else about him that seemed to be able to captivate all he came in contact with. It was those pale gold eyes that burned yellow when angry. A pair that were deep set and framed by dark, thick slashes of prominent brows. Those high cut cheekbones that created shadows at the sides of his face, matching his slim nose, pointed chin and dark, long curly hair.

He wore a dark grey slashed doublet, a wide reticella lace collar and cuffs, complete with a black broadbrimmed hat. Oh, and those all-important farting crackers, a term I had invented to describe breeches that had caught on and was now widely used… a proud moment for me as I liked to think of myself as somewhat of a wordsmith.

"What took you so long?" he snapped, and practically dragged me out of the carriage as the coachman was unstrapping my trunk, and one that admittedly was starting to smell a bit. I yanked my arm from his hold and looked up at him, with my hand to my hip between the cream doublet and the skirt that fringed it.

"I have been travelling for months and that's the first thing you say to me!" I snapped back, and the moment I saw that evil gleam in his eyes, I knew if we hadn't been out in public I would currently be suffering from a sore cheek… and be grinding my teeth to hold myself back from kicking this man to the ground. Of course, Pan wasn't without his powers, in fact, he was pretty much the original snake charmer, for he was never found without pipes tucked away in his pocket.

Honestly, I was pretty sure that he had put some sort of spell on me when I had started to argue about taking on this job in the first place. Because before I knew anything else, I was on a ship heading out of Britannia and on my way to the Middle East. Well, now that I was back and he had taken possession of my cargo, I felt a huge weight lift from my mind. It had been like a mental veil had been shrouded around me this entire time. I even found myself shaking my body as if I was trying to rid myself of the lingering remains of his suggestive mind.

"Why do I feel like you have been controlling me, Pan?" I asked the moment this feeling left me. He sneered down at me and took hold of the top of my arm, before digging his fingers into my flesh hard enough to make me wince.

"Now is not the time, now come, my Flittermouse," he said, which was his pet name for me, and something he had heard his friend, Playwright, Ben Jonson say a time or two. Personally, it just made me grit my teeth and wonder why I ever used to find the term endearing. Actually, I was starting to think that there weren't many endearing facts about Pan left.

After this he quickly commandeered another carriage, and I found myself moaning in exasperation at finding myself unable once more to have the opportunity to stretch my legs. I swear, any longer and I would forget how to use them all together!

"Are we going to your lodgings?"

"No, not until the job is done," he answered, looking from beyond the curtain, as if eager to get to wherever it was we were heading now. But this was the moment that Percival started squeaking in my leather satchel, and Pan turned to look at me in shock.

"Really, Winifred, you kept one on your person?"

"But of course, he is my favourite and I have named

him Percival." I watched as he rolled his eyes in disgust but for once he refrained from saying anything, although I think that was most likely because we had arrived.

"Put that thing away and try not to embarrass me again!" he said before removing himself from the carriage, therefore missing the way I placed the tip of my thumb behind my front teeth and flicked it forward at him.

"Come on, Percival, let's get this whiffle-whaffle over with," I said, before tucking him back in the bag and giving him a little scratch behind the ear. Then I followed Pan out of the carriage and frowned up at the sight that met me.

"What are we doing here?" I asked, standing in front of the Church of St Peter upon Cornhill, which stood on the highest point of the City of London. One that currently looked to be in the middle of morning mass.

It also had to be said that for this demonic Imp, standing outside a church wouldn't have been my first choice of places to be. But then, even when here as a foreigner, all good Protestants would of course attend their local parish church in London, just as they would at home.

Yawn.

I would much prefer to be eating marchpane or gingerbread for a pennyworth. But then, all my kind still had to take care when hiding our true selves, for if it was discovered you didn't attend Church, then everyone would know, and news would get to the authorities in this self-policing society. England was, after all, still at war with Spain and the Pope. Which meant the authorities were still on the alert for Jesuit missionaries and Spanish agents. So basically, you didn't dare go near the lodgings of the ambassador of a Catholic prince on Sunday, as it would have been assumed you were going to hear mass.

But like I said... yawn, yawn, yawn.

For I couldn't think of a better cure to a sleepless time. Just like if there was an event of national importance to justify a special service led by the Queen, a mass of fools was always found trying to gain entry to St Paul's Cathedral. The cathedral itself had never really recovered from being struck by lightning in 1561, and it needed a lot of work doing to it. And in regard to the Queen, well, then I doubted she would be attending again, for it was rumoured the Queen's days were numbered. Which made me wonder if Pan's next plot at causing mayhem had to anything to do with it. Because if she was as sickly as it sounded, then my chance at checking out the royal tiltyard on Accession Day jousts, in the Queen's presence, wasn't going to happen.

But then it had been rumoured, the death of the Queenie's dearest friend, had sent her into a severe depression.

Pan had sent a letter on to one of the ports he knew I would be travelling through, with instructs and news of what was happening back in England. In February 1603, there happened the death of Catherine Carey, the Countess of Nottingham, who was the niece of the Queen's cousin. She had been in attendance at court and with the Queen for 44 years. In fact, since the beginning of March, Pan said that Elizabeth was said to be found sat motionless on a cushion for hours on end. I couldn't help but wonder myself what it would feel like to have a friend that impacted my life that way. Someone I loved so much that the loss would bring me closer to death because of a broken heart. I had tried to play the mortal card for a while, and felt the pain of having them die hit me enough to want to leave. But I had never discovered the type of love that felt bound to my very soul.

Which made me ask, was it possible for a mortal to die of a broken heart? Yes, I believed so, but the question I often asked myself, was if it was possible for an immortal to find death in the same way? Of course, I was getting ahead of myself, seeing as I knew that I had not yet experienced what it felt like to be truly in love.

But more importantly…

To be loved in return.

SEVEN

MY FIRST BAD

25TH MARCH 1603

L ove.
    I had been blind.

My eyes automatically cast sideways to Pan, who I knew had tried to manipulate me into believing that what we had together was love. But love didn't come with a beating or a closed fist, and I may not have yet experienced it myself, but it didn't take a genius like Archimedes to understand it. Which brought me back to now, and wondering exactly what it was we were doing stood outside of a church during mass, one that was teeming with people. Because in this particular area of London, it was one of the most popular with residents and of course, if you weren't found in church then you were most likely going to be shunned.

"Hey, what are you doing?" I shouted the moment he grabbed the trunk and started dragging it closer to doors.

"What does it look like? I'm getting paid to do a job," he snapped, before slamming down the case so that it popped open and out poured all twenty rats. Naturally, they started to fan out in different directions, no doubt trying to seek shelter.

This was when it was confirmed... *I had been his puppet, yet again.*

Gods, but I was stupid.

"Pan! Please don't hurt them!" I shouted, when he pulled his weapon of choice from beneath his long jacket and soon started to play. I found myself wincing and tensing from the sound. As for mortal ears, they would have believed it was nothing more than a sweet melody played by someone in hopes to be tossed a coin their way for the effort. But little did they know what it truly was.

It was a death call.

I knew it down to my core. Gods, just how blind and foolish had he made me? Had it really all been a lie, one

I had been living through for hundreds of years? Had he really had the power to veil my conscience and shroud it in darkness for so long? What had I become?

"No… no don't listen to him… come back, my friends… come back!" I tried to shout, to communicate with them, when all the rats stopped in their tracks and scurried back to him as if he was now their master. But then I felt the rustling in the bag next to me, as even Percival was caught under his spell. So, I quickly grabbed him and held him to my chest, stroking him and cooing down at him,

"Ssshh… calm and do not listen, my friend… don't listen to the evil inside of him," I said, before putting him back in my bag and tying the cord tighter so he couldn't escape. As for Pan, he continued to play as he walked up the steps towards the church.

I had no idea why he deemed it important enough to get the rats to follow him inside, and prayed to the Gods that it was nothing more than jest on his part. But then it seemed like an awful lot of effort when he could quite easily have found rats here. No, I couldn't be naive any longer. I couldn't allow the doubt he planted to take root. Because I knew there was something about this that wasn't right. Which meant I had a very bad feeling about what would happen when I discovered the truth.

Pan and the rats soon disappeared inside, the sight of which would not have caused even a flinch, for these days seeing a rat was a common occurrence. In fact, it was almost like the equivalent of seeing one's neighbour passing by. But then again, a man leading a small army of them behind him, now surely that would have been an eye opener for anyone… unless of course he was hiding the sight from mortals with his control?

In truth, if I hadn't been so desperate and in need of money, then I would have turned around and left with Percival. But the simple fact remained, for the journey had left me near penniless. And unless I was willing to pickpocket those who were just as unfortunate as I, then I had to wait to get paid for the job that I had done. Which meant when Pan came back out with not a single rat in sight, I knew the job had been done.

So, as he approached, tucking his pipe back into his jacket, I found myself stepping from side to side nervously, with my internal hope playing out in my mind,

'Please pay me, please pay me, please pay me… Gods, I bet you he doesn't pay me,' but then added to this was another hope…

'Please let this act not hurt the innocent.'

"Do I want to know what that was all about?" I couldn't help but snap. Something he didn't like, as I soon found his hand at my throat in a bruising hold.

"Not if you want to keep your pretty little head," he answered, telling me I was close to igniting his anger, yet I was a fool, hence why I bit back.

"And what is that supposed to mean?"

"Precisely what it sounds like, now do you want to get paid or not?" he snarled like some angry dog. Then he dropped my neck and grabbed me by the top of my arm before I could fall. After this, he led me near the south porch where I could see someone waiting for us. This happened concurrently with people starting to exit morning mass, and it seemed as if it had been planned this way, so as not to arouse suspicion on our meeting.

For even I knew that these were perilous times, as England was still being torn in two. This was ever since Henry VIII caused the Church of England to break away from the authority of the Pope and the Roman Catholic Church, all so he could annul his first marriage. Which meant that even years later and long after his death, two religions were still butting heads like bulls as the Catholics and Protestants fought for dominance. This became even more so, for people knew that at the end of Queen Elizabeth's reign, it would be the end of the Tudors, for she was known as the Virgin Queen for a reason.

Now, did I believe it was because she was a prude and had never felt the pleasure of a man between her legs? No, I did not. I believed that the reason Elizabeth didn't take a husband was that she did not want anyone to be known as king. She didn't want to become a slave to a man and cast her rule in the shadow of such a title, when men still dominated the world above that of women.

But this also meant, no heir to the throne and the reign of the Tudors coming to an end, and with it suspicion of who should take the throne other than James I, her sister Mary Queen of Scots' son. With him, came the fear that the Scottish would then overrule England, for no one in this place wanted to see a Scot on the throne. As for myself, I couldn't give two cute owl hoots which pompous, lavishly dressed bottom sat itself on such a chair, for I had my own royalty to worry about... and they were a damn sight scarier than any mortal monarch could bestow.

A fear that grew increasingly worrisome as I had a feeling that we were meddling in mortal history, and that was a dangerous game indeed. Because if we were ever found guilty by the King of Kings, well, those crimes were punishable by death... *of the everlasting kind.* Dominic Draven was the immortal leader for all those of my kind, of all the supernatural existence that resided on Earth. In short, he was one scary, brutal king that couldn't be swayed by a greased palm.

In other words, we were fucked if we were caught meddling in mortal life in a way that impacted the future. Hence why I took more nervous steps, stumbling due to the rough treatment of Pan and his unyielding hold on me. However, the closer we got to the south porch, the more I could sense that whoever we were meeting was a mortal... and not one of our kind.

"Did you do it, did you do as was promised to me?" the man, who was no more than in his forties, asked. He donned a white wig and had jowls like a large dog.

"They have been released, and as we speak scratching their hides amongst English limbs," Pan answered with a dangerous smirk, making me frown.

"What is that supposed to mean?" I questioned, knowing he was talking about the rats, and wondered what it meant that they were scratching themselves amongst the mortals. Both men then sneered at me, before the man in the shadows gave me an appreciative look up and down, and said,

"And who is this young filly, for clear it be she is no boy?" I rolled my eyes but was stopped from answering as Pan did so for me, and not in a nice way.

"She's no one, a mere tool, and one I used to acquire what was needed to get the job done." I huffed at this but knew to hold my tongue, for we were out of sight and therefore I was unprotected by the witness of others.

"Well, I would like to use her as a tool for my cock." I scrunched up my nose in disgust, knowing that if he came anywhere near me with that thing, I would snap it off in a second. I didn't know what it was about my disgusted look that pleased him, but he seemed happy about it.

"Yes, well that will cost you extra, but as for now, you know what I require." I huffed at this and looked up at Pan in utter shock! I mean yes, he hadn't exactly been the best champion of mine, but he had never been willing to prostitute me before.

Oh yes, it was time to let Pan go alright, and right after he placed coin in my hand I was getting out of London for good… before the shit fell amongst the cobble and I ended up Kickerapoo.

"I acquired the Oracle stones, yes," the man said, making my jaw drop in shock.

"Pan," I said his name in warning for this was bad, as in extremely so. Upon the word of the Gods, we were dabbling in forces far from our depth, and the seriousness of my situation had hit me like a King's guard. What the Hell's hounds had Pan gotten me into this time?!

"Silence your tongue! Now, hand me the stones as was promised." The man nodded and pulled the leather pouch from his waist before handing it over to Pan, who was quickly tugging at the cord.

"It came with a warning but alas I cannot fathom a reason beyond one of superstition."

"Tell me!" Pan demanded as he tipped the four different coloured moonstones onto his hand, making me gasp at the sight of them, for I had heard the part they would play in the prophecy and who they were destined for... all my kind had.

The King's Electus.

His mortal Chosen One, and one destined to change our worlds entwined. By the Gods what had Pan been thinking for this wasn't just a death sentence, this was a sentence handed down by the Devil himself!

This was the reason I started to step away from them both before Pan grabbed me and yanked me back, snarling down,

"You go nowhere, Flittermouse." Then he nodded for the mystery man to continue.

"The witch I acquired them from told me that there are only four times such moonstones can be used, and if you miss one opportunity then hundreds of years will pass before the next moon is right, for the power of creation and binding will only be awakened after each phase lights the sky," he said, in a way that you could tell that even he didn't understand it and why would he... he was mortal.

"The comet will soon light the skies and reveal its first opportunity," Pan said, with wide eyes full of greed and dark intent as he gazed down at his treasure. So, this had been his plan all along, and I had been nothing but a tool to use just like this little prick in front of us. We were all tools for the using in Pan's eyes. Well, I was done and as soon as I could, I was getting far away from this Devil walker, for he was about to come far too close to knocking on Hell's door and dancing with death.

"Now, how do I know your side of the bargain will be

kept?" the man asked, making Pan snap out of his trance. He slid the stones back into the leather pouch and told him,

"When the smell of burning bodies fills the air once more, of course." At this, I covered my mouth as a shocking gasp slipped free. The true horror of what I had been used for started to take shape.

"No... Gods, no," I muttered, just before the church bells started ringing, interrupting my shock, and the second of three told us precisely what it was before shouting in the streets could be heard...

A death knell.

"Hear ye, hear ye, the Queen is dead! The Queen is dead, for London will mourn!" This was added to a bell rung by the town crier, before people started whispering about her dying in her bed during the night, whilst others stood frozen in shock with tears running down their faces.

"Good lord, it really happened, just as you said it would by killing the countess," the man said, making me start shaking my head. Gods, but they had even killed Catherine Carey, the Queen's dearest friend.

"Love has the power to break people, Watson, just as I said it would," Pan said with a grin, and I couldn't help but think this referred to me also, because hadn't that been what he had been trying to do to me?

"Then it is time," the man I now knew was named Watson said, making Pan agree.

"That it is, and now you know what to do."

"That surely be, for what you said has come to pass, and now I will head to Scotland and ensure my position by being the one to announce such to the new King of England, assuring James that I am loyal to his party. Once this begins, so does the plot to take them all, King and Parliament combined," he said, telling me of his plan as if I wasn't even here any longer and was of no coincidence to either of them, for I had already played my part.

"The plague will arise once more and therefore give you time, as his royal coronation will be delayed due to the increase of death among London. For by the time they're through, this cesspool of death will be the very last place he will want to find himself."

"I hope you are right," Watson said, making me clear my throat and say,

"Oh no, Pan, what have you done... what does this have to do with us?" I asked, after seeing a black rat scurry past like a sign or bad omen.

"How do you think the plague is spread, you stupid

girl!" Pan sneered, and then he too looked towards the rat, confirming my biggest fears... I had caused another outbreak of the plague. Which was when I too realised it must have been carried by rats...

By rats from the East.

This was when tears started to emerge before running freely down my face. Then I looked back at all the people who had emerged from the church, now mourning the death of their Queen. Knowing pretty soon they would have so much more to mourn, like the death of their loved ones, before they too would fall with those I had unknowingly allowed Pan to infect.

"Gods... what have I done," I uttered in revulsion at my own foolish actions.

"Exactly what I have commanded of you," Pan said, pausing long enough to spin me around and yank me back against his chest. Then he grabbed my breast from behind and squeezed it painfully, before whispering at my back...

"You've been bad for me... just like I knew you would..."

"My Bad, Little Imp."

EIGHT

ON THE RUN
PRESENT DAY

"Oh no, Wantie Pip, what did you do?" The sweet little voice of Amelia asked me, after I had finished an edited version of my story. Because, well let's face it, she was three going on four after all, and didn't need to know the gruesome details of my past. So, I had spent a great deal of time going into detail about Percival, a part she had enjoyed most of all.

Man, but I missed that little guy.

"You mean after the bad man Meanie Bo Beanie Pan, threw me under a bus?" I replied, making her gasp in horror.

STEPHANIE HUDSON

"He threw you under a bus as well!?" At this, I smiled down at her and said,

"Not exactly, Treacle. It's an expression that means he double crossed me, basically a bit like when Mandy at preschool tried to get you into trouble for writing on the wall."

"And it wasn't me!" she shouted, now getting the comparison, and feeling the injustice... a hard lesson indeedio.

"I know, Baby Doll, she was mean, like PanMan," I added, brushing back her hair and getting more paint on it.

"Bonkers Conkers... that's not nice... he's worse than Skeletor," she said, making me grin knowing how much I was rubbing off on her.

"I think you're right, Pickle," I replied after she referred to one of my favourite 80s TV programmes, He-Man, which naturally, I had on box set. Oh, and yes, but of course, it was a series I had made her sit through. But then again, I had a sweet shop in my room, so it was easy to lure in little children and force them to be my friend and sit with me during these times. Besides, I had already made Adam watch it about 80 gazillion times already, which meant I knew he was hitting his limit.

"What happen next?" she asked, rubbing her forearm along her chin as the paint there was annoying her and making a blue streak smear its way across her skin. I should probably mention, at this point we were currently writing my sorry note across a whole wall in our bedroom. Of course, I had to first paint over the giant rainbow that framed a graffiti mural I had done of our history together. Our history I was leaving, but the rainbow part had to go if I was to fit in my 'sorry, please still love me' note.

As for my story, well, I had told her most of this whilst we let the white part dry, saying bye-bye to the rainbow. We had also had tea and biscuits served to us by an Oompa Loompa. Or at least I had tried to do this, but let's just say animatronics only went so far and didn't deal well with boiling water. Hence, I had to take over in that chore and gave Little Bean one that had more milk than tea in it, so it was only lukewarm.

As for mine, well I had added a full chocolate digestive biscuit to my cup, instead of sugar, and was using a spoon to eat the floating lumpy soggy bits from the top. Amelia found this hilarious, especially whenever I did it in front of her mother, Toots, who looked close to making the sign of the cross in front of her at the sight of the abomination I had created by ruining the sacred English tea her husband made sure she was never in short supply of.

But we had finished the tea and biscuits and we were currently mixing coloured paints. Amelia had decided to be in charge of the blue hearts to show how upset we were that he had not yet forgiven us.

I say us, but it was really more of a 'me' thing. Because, of course, Amelia had done nothing wrong, and just like that time back in 1603...

I was the one in trouble.

YE OLDE CHESHIRE CHEESE
1ST SEPTEMBER 1603

"Another!" I heard shouted from the table next to me, as a meaty hand hit down an empty clay tankard interrupting Polly, who sounded like an angel as she sung, 'My Jolly Sailor Bold'. It was a pretty but sad shanty that was said to be a favourite sung all around the seas, by the kings that commanded them... *Pirates.*

"I wouldn't have given up three thousand a year for cock!" one man said in jest, regarding the words pretty Polly sung, whereas his friend retorted back,

"Aye, and nay there be a filly that would pay a shilling fay ye cock!" He laughed, making others join in, and I picked up my own tankard of ale just before the man was punched off his chair and landed into my table. Then, once he staggered back to his feet, I kicked my table back in place, took a substantial glug and placed my drink down as I continued to listen to the song.

It was true, I had been in hiding, but I had hit my limit in needing a drink and only had enough coin left for one more night's stay in the city. Hence, why I found myself in the Cheese, a pub that had been serving drinks at 145 Fleet Street, on Wine Office Court since 1538. In truth, far beneath the cellars and foundations of this building was a rabbit warren of caverns and large caves that were big enough they could have housed castles, for it was like a hidden city down there.

I knew this thanks to the supernatural force that had once lived there over a thousand years ago. But it had long since been left abandoned, and over time a city had grown above its lost treasures with its mortal inhabitants having not a dicky about its existence. And what could I say... I was a creature of habit coming back here time and time again.

Now as for the man, Watson, and why he and his band of co-conspirators had wanted another plague epidemic to hit once the Queen had died, had been simple. It had been done to try and prevent the King from coming here for his coronation. They had managed this for a while but not in preventing James from actually coming to London. Therefore, it was said that their next plan had been to have James surprised and seized somewhere. But then this didn't work, as slighted and rebuffed drunken fools often had loose and loud tongues. Which meant that while the fopdoodles (which was another word I could claim to have created) spoke loudly about their plans in capturing the Tower of London, converting the King to Catholicism and making Watson Lord Keeper, they were overheard and betrayed to the King.

This led to Watson being captured in August at Hay-on-Wye on the Welsh border. I had heard rumours that this plot had been just the beginning, for something bigger was coming. A plot so big that it had the power to reshape English history, they said, and that its parliament and royalty would fall.

Something to do with…

Gunpowder.

But like most things in this city, these were merely whispers. However, as Watson's execution drew near, those whispers grew into something deeper and far more serious than simply trying to manipulate a King.

But as far as I was concerned, the gobermouch (again, one of mine) was getting what was coming to him. Now, as for me, well I had no choice but to reach out to one of my contacts to try and secure a passage off this damn island, back to where I knew I had more of a chance at disappearing for good.

Back to my conkers… *My own Realm.*

Because I had run from my arrest and skipped out on my trial, one I knew that I would be found guilty at. For I knew that the King of Kings wanted to hold someone accountable for the loss of mortal life that had swept the city these last six months. Of course, Pan was in the wind, but not before he had given me up to the authorities, doing so quicker than I could say, black rat come back. Because, as I had been busy questioning why Pan hadn't taken the journey himself, he had been plotting this from the beginning. He had me believing his spoken word on the matter that it was too dangerous for him to travel, due to being wanted man.

But well, this hadn't been entirely true.

For like I said, Pan had a plan from the beginning. This plan being that there would be many witnesses to me travelling with a trunk starting back all the way from the east. A woman dressed like a man had something to hide and only looked more guilty, but as an Imp, well doing such only more so.

But as for Pan, he had only a few mortal minds to control to wipe free any sight of him. Meaning the bastard had set me up to take the fall for this from the very start. So, as I was being hunted, he had quickly taking his loot and fled the city.

However, this wasn't before a few things happened, one in particular that utterly broke my heart. This had been after I had threatened to go to the King himself and explain what Pan had done. I knew this would have come with a beating at the very least, but I had been hoping it was enough of a threat that he would have the power to call back the rats, and therefore potentially save thousands before the spread could make it too far. Of course, he got a great deal of pleasure in telling me it was too late now. Alas the mortals didn't yet know it but the fleas that lived amongst the rats were the ones that spread the Black Death, and had already jumped and started biting their new hosts, infecting them.

I questioned how Pan knew any of this, but he mainly gave me that sadistic grin of his before he acted with violent intent. It had been right after Watson, that dick pincher, had disappeared that Pan had grabbed the front of my doublet and dragged me closer to his face, telling me,

"To underestimate me, is to die!" Then, before I could stop him, he reached in the leather bag that I held Percival in, took hold of him and crushed him to death in his fist before tossing him aside.

"NO!" I screamed, before running to where he'd landed and scooping up his broken little body, praying it wasn't too late... *but it was.*

He had killed my little Percival.

"Wwwhy... why would you do this... why would you do this to me?!" I sobbed from where I hunched over, holding him to my chest... my friend... *my only friend.*

"It's simple really, I needed someone gullible enough and easy to manipulate, and well, I do enjoy a good tight cunt to fuck in the meantime." I winced at this before turning my head away in disgust.

"I meant nothing to you," I muttered in pain and even

as I said it, I wished I could have taken it back, for he merely laughed at me.

"You mean to me the same as that rat you hold in your hands, along with the rest of the population. You were a carrier, a tool to be used and nothing more, for I have everything I need…" He paused long enough to lean down on a bent knee to deliver his last words closer to me.

"… and soon, word will reach the King of who planned this and who is to be blamed for it all."

"No…" I whispered as panic started to mix with my grief.

"Yes… and whilst they are chasing you through this mortal cesspool of shit, I will be sailing away with plans of resurrection. For the King of Kings' days are numbered, as there will soon be someone more powerful taking his throne."

"You will never get away with this," I uttered, even if my voice sounded too small to back up the threat. Hence why he just laughed before taking hold of my chin and forcing my face cruelly back to his, where my hatred for him could be seen in my watery gaze.

"It was a shame, little Flittermouse… you would have made a good footstool at the end of my throne!" At this

I could stand it no longer, I got up and punched my fist downwards across his face before taking him to the floor as I wrestled him to the ground, doing so with far more purpose than just anger.

Of course, I knew I was no match for Pan for I had laid witness to his strength many times before, and I was not exactly a pushover Pansy. In truth, I really had no idea who Pan was, as it had become clear that everything I had once believed had been planted like a baby sapling taking root. Years and years of being manipulated into believing whatever he wanted me to believe. There had been no truth in my life for these past few hundred years with him.

I had been a colossal fool.

And now my greatest crime of this foolishness would end up being at the expense of mortal lives. A disease I loathed more than any other before it had come back to haunt me. Which meant that I would once again find myself running from it, along with trying to escape the punishment in paying for Pan's crimes.

So, yes, in that moment I fought and without much care, for I felt as if I had little choice left. I needed something. Just one thing that I knew had the potential to aid me in my redemption. One last fuck you to an enemy I hadn't known

I had been in bed with all these years!

As predicted, Pan subdued me quite easily, and I was knocked off him with a punch to the face that I could feel had dislocated my jaw. Then, once there on the floor and at his mercy, he rained down punch after punch until eventually, I blacked out.

But in doing so, I gave way to the darkness with one single comfort in mind.

I was a thief and a bloody good one at that.

Which meant that comfort came from what I held tightly in my fist under my back...

The Moonstones.

NINE

TRAPPED, CAUGHT AND... *SENTENCED*
YE OLDE CHESHIRE CHEESE
1ST SEPTEMBER 1603

A bloody good thief... *that was me.*

Now, exactly when it was that Pan discovered he had a bag full of rocks, I didn't know, but the pebbles I had picked up whilst consoling myself on the death of my friend had been my plan after seeing him die. Then I let the anger burn bright as I had taken him to the ground, doing so as the distraction needed to make the switch. In truth, I had been surprised to find myself waking in the dirt with rain dripping on my face... and my little fist still holding the Oracle's Moonstones.

After this, I decided to get my skinny body moving and myself lost in London, in case Pan discovered my trickery and gave me a beating I wouldn't be coming back from. So, I had clicked my jaw back into place and limped my way to another part of the city, taking Percival with me so I could bury him somewhere nice in this shit hole.

And now here I was...

"There is nothing that can console me, but my jolly sailor bold." Polly sang the last line with heart wrenching sadness, and I felt the tears roll down my cheeks as I picked up my tankard, and whispered,

"To Percival, may you be in Rat Heaven." Then I wiped my wet lips with the back of my hand and placed my empty tankard down, just as the doors opened and in walked trouble. I had my back to the door, but I just knew the moment I felt a shiver wrack my body that my own kind had entered. So, I released a sigh and let my feet, that had been resting on the table, fall to the floor. Then I stood, rolled a shoulder, and cracked my neck to the side, getting ready for the fight before I said,

"Alright pikelets, who wants an ass kicking this time?" Then I turned around and the moment the entire room fell to the floor unconscious, I knew I was in big donkey shit. But then I raised my eyes up to the masterly figure and I couldn't help it, my mouth dropped open. Because there, standing right in front of me was none other than the King himself!

Gods in Heaven and Hell combined, the man could burn the feathered bloomers off a chicken! He was so large he made Pan look like a beanpole, for he had muscles that only existed on the Gods themselves! Long black hair was tied back from his handsome face, one that was only revealed fully when he removed his wide brimmed hat, making me suck in a quick breath.

"Oh, Lordy and mercy be." Dark eyes, that gleamed purple with a spark of power ignited in their depths, narrowed before a single dark brow raised in question at my reaction to him.

"Winifred Ambrogetti, I presume," his strong deep voice said with a nod in my direction, and the moment I opened my mouth to speak the words erupted like Mount Vesuvius.

"I didn't do it!" At this, the King smirked before raising his hat back and repositioning it with both hands as he said,

"I see." Then the last thing I uttered before he clicked

his fingers and I met darkness, was a damning,

"Ah fuck!"

LOCATION UNKNOWN...

The next time I started to come to, I knew something was different for I was no longer waking in my own lodgings. An obvious fact, as for one, it was warm, and my attic room had never been warm... *not once*. I also felt comfort in the form of a bed with coverings, and not just hard slats of wood and straw filled sacks.

I could also hear the crackling of a fire, along with feeling its warmth on my skin and I swear, had my mind not been screaming at me to wake, then I would have snuggled further into my comfort and promptly fallen back to sleep. But knowing of my different surroundings, it was clear that the King himself had taken me and brought me to his current place of residence, wherever that may be.

So, I opened my eyes and confirmed my suspicions when taking in such luxury. The large room was covered in dark oak panelling and some modern touches, such as arches and pilasters. But these architectural elements, that were used to give the appearance of a supporting column and to articulate an extent of wall, weren't widely used as of yet.

They were rarely seen in England, for it was a fashion from ancient Greek and Roman architecture and had been adopted by the Italians of late. Just like the caryatids, that were beautifully sculptured female figures, and were currently holding up the large marble lintel over the fireplace. These female figures were serving as an architectural support, taking the place of a column or a pillar, supporting an entablature on their pretty heads. The Greek term karyatides literally meant 'maidens of Karyai', an ancient town on the Peloponnese and where this design originated from.

It was one of the grandest rooms I had ever been in, with its lush thick fabrics and expensive silks, all in the richest of sunset colours. Even the ceilings were outfitted with ornate plasterwork and illusionistic paintings, offering a contrast to the daring wood carvings that embellished the windows and doors. And in the centre of it all was me, sat in huge four poster bed, and facing the large fireplace that held a roaring fire taking the chill off this huge room.

"You're finally awake." I heard a voice I had never heard before, but the moment my eyes took in the beauty sat off to one side, I knew instantly who it was.

Sophia Draven, *sister to the King.*

"Your majesty," I said, taking in her lovely face that reminded me of Aphrodite, the ancient Greek Goddess of sexual love and beauty. Dark ebony hair just like her brother, was coiled artfully up and framed by her heart shaped head dress studded with pearls and jewels. Natural red lips grinned at me as dark eyes gleamed with mirth. Her slight frame was covered in a deep-red velvet gown embroidered with gold leaves, and long hanging sleeves. It had a fitted bodice with a wide ankle-length skirt, worn over what was most likely a cartwheel frame. I could also see her shoes to match had a high wooden heel and showed a clear sign of money. But then everything about this scene screamed riches of the likes I had never known, and suddenly I felt like a slumbegger in the presence of royalty.

Yet she simply waved her jewel covered hand at me and said,

"Enough of all that now, for you and I are about embark on a friendship of mutual understanding." I frowned in question before being honest in my answer.

"We are?"

"Do you want to survive?" she asked bluntly in return.

"Very much so."

"Then, if that be the fact, I will ensure the ruling is not death." At this, I sat up straighter and almost shouted with glee,

"You will!?" She bowed her head gracefully, and said,

"I will, but alas, I will require something in return." At this, my shoulders slumped knowing now there was a price.

"And that is?" I asked in a tone reserved for one of disappointment.

"Mostly on your part, I can imagine it will be silence." Okay, so now I was really confused.

"I am afraid I do not understand, my lady."

"Yes, and I'm starting to wonder if that not be more preferable but alas the Oracle has entrusted me with this task, and it will not be one I will fail at," she replied cryptically.

"The Oracle, Pythia?" I asked, with my tone turning to a higher pitch, instantly putting my hand in my pocket and taking hold of the stones I kept on me at all times.

"You know of her?" Sophia asked, making swallow hard before skimming over my answer with a veil of truth that couldn't be denied.

"Forgive me, my lady, but all our kind know of the Oracle of Delphi."

"Well, she knows of you and apparently, the importance you will play." Her answer was shocking.

"Me!?" At this she simply nodded and I, in turn, shook my head before saying,

"Forgive me again, my lady, but are you sure you have not mistaken me for someone else, for I am far from important." She granted me a soft grace of her eyes before she told me,

"Do not be so hasty to pollute your person, for as you know the Fates are never wrong and if what the Oracle says is true, then you will indeed play a great and powerful part in the future." I released a sigh, only wishing this were true but really, what I said was the truth, for I was a no one in both the mortal realm and that of my own. I was a split seed growing from the wrong side. A lost one even before my birth.

What could I do to aid the Fates?

"And what part would that be?" I asked, unable to hold back any longer.

"The part of knowing my brother's Chosen One and being of great use to his Electus." At this, I sucked in a shuddered breath before I let it go again on a whoosh of air.

"I...I... mercy be... I am not sure you have the right Imp, my lady, I seem to be nothing more than destined for trouble."

"And how do you know that's not exactly what she will need?" Sophia Draven answered with a smirk and a playful wink.

"So does this mean that your brother is going to let me off the charges set against me?" At this she laughed and said,

"Good Gods, no, you were the cause of over 30,000 mortal deaths, this is not something that we can let sink into the River Thames and let lie amongst the silt." This time, I released a hopeless sigh before allowing my head to fall forward.

"Well, I guess it is better than being one of those dead bodies hauled out of the Thames each week," I commented drily, making her laugh.

"Yes, well that's what King Henry III gets for letting a pet polar bear swim there to catch his fish, they are likely to catch something else instead... foolish being," she said, making me laugh as it was true. Back in 1252 the King received the white bear as a gift from King of Norway, that he kept in the Tower of London... when it wasn't being allowed to swim in the river, obviously.

"So, what will happen to me then?" I asked, getting back to more important factors of this conversation, like that of my life and what was to become of it.

"You will serve your time in Hell, I imagine, but have no fear, for I have reached out to my father in hopes he will intervene when the decision is made on where they will place you and the punishment they decide. You should have his protection and I can only hope this is enough." I had to say, this didn't fill me a with donkey cart full of confidence.

"But why not tell the King of my importance, for if the Oracle has deemed it so, then surely, he should..." This is where she cut me off, doing so with a wave of her hand before speaking.

"As you know, the Fates do not work like that, for anything my brother knows could impact the future, including you, little Imp." Another sigh released and a question to follow.

"So, the King knows nothing of this?" I asked.

"No one does but you and I." It was at this point that she

came over and sat on the edge of the bed before releasing her own sigh.

"Ever since the day my brother heard of the existence of his Chosen One, his obsession began, whereas my own was destined to follow, for I have been charged by the Oracle and the very Fates themselves to become a guardian of sorts," she told me gently.

"A guardian?"

"A watcher, and keeper over a prophecy so important, that it will shape this world unlike any other has ever done before it." I nodded in understanding. For all of my kind had heard of this fated event, as it was said there were even those that wanted to prevent it and therefore potentially see the fall of the Gods once more.

"And how do we achieve something like this, what are we destined to do?" I found myself asking yet again, for that was my place in this conversation.

"It is said that the Chosen One will seek out my brother, despite his constant searching. For it will only happen when the time has come and deemed right by the Fates," she replied, with a shake of her head as if recalling all the King had done in his search.

"And the part you are to play, what of that?"

"I am to be the one to recognise her, even before my brother, and it is said that I am to play an integral part in putting her in his path and setting her on the right line of fate."

"And me, what of my fate in all this?" I asked again, just needing to be sure that I wasn't to be some worm dangling on the end of a hook.

"You will play a different role in her fate, that is all I know," she replied, making me hope my involvement in this girl's life was as a friend and not a foe, for that would not bode well for me.

"So, we will work together?" At this, she gave me a genuine smile and her face lit up with such beauty it almost stole my breath.

"I believe you and I will become good friends, Imp, but until then, you must serve out your sentence for your crimes."

"But it wasn't just me who did this, I was manipulated, there was a man, his name was Pan and he tricked me," I started to say but the King's sister simply shook her head.

"I'm afraid even if this is true, it will not stop the damnation of your act for I'm afraid the sentence has too been fated, for the Oracle told me that no matter what you say to me now, nothing should change the outcome of your sentence for the crimes against mortal life." At this my eyes widened so much they almost hurt.

"But that is unjust... I don't understand, why..." I started, but once more she held a hand up and interrupted my agreement against what she was deeming be my fate.

"Again, I am but a messenger of the Fates, and it is a task I have held for thousands of years without even my brother's knowledge to this point. Sure, he knows of my interest, but he believes this to be purely for a solicitous reason. One born from a sister who wishes for their brother's happiness and nothing more. He does not know the true depth of my involvement or the imperative burden which I bear," she said, giving my hand a squeeze in comfort as I lowered my head in defeat.

"And now?" I asked in a small voice that only spoke of her own victory.

"And now I am not alone in my task, for there will come a time when you will sit by my side and we will converse together as friends." Now this certainly got my attention as my head snapped up so fast, had she been any closer I might have connected with her chin.

"We will?!" She laughed, clearly amused by my enthusiasm.

"Yes, after all, it is fated also." Hearing this, I finally allowed myself to smile, for if it was fated to be then at the very least my sentence would end and most importantly, I would survive it. So, I decided to focus on this positive fact and tell her with honesty,

"I've never really had a friend, only of the mortal kind once, but that was long ago and we all know how that ends." At this point she placed her hand on my shoulder and gave me a comforting pat, before telling me,

"Then consider this the beginning and something new for both of us. But first, as friends, I believe I should know what you prefer to be called."

"Pipper, or Pip for short," I said with a grin, and she smiled back at return.

"All right, then Pip it is, and in turn you may call me Sophia. Now

let's see what we can do about getting you in the right side of Hell and in making your punishment a little easier." I released a big sigh, making my lips quiver before I started nodding, now accepting the inevitable. But still I found myself asking just to be sure,

"And what of the King... what if he decides something else?"

"Leave my brother to me. Trust me, if there's one thing I have mastered after all these years being his sister, it is how to manipulate him into doing what I require... I believe you can call it being a nag."

"I invented that word you know." At this she laughed and said,

"I have a feeling it will catch on."

"Now, are you ready, my friend?" she asked, and I had to be honest in my answer.

"Is anyone ever really ready to be sentenced to a prison in Hell?" Sophia winked and said,

"Only when the warden is the Devil you know."

TEN

PUNISHMENT AND LUST
PRESENT DAY

"Oh no, you got sent to Hell prison?!" Little Bean shouted, now covering her mouth with both hands and getting even more paint on her face, and that was saying something considering there was a lot already on there.

Of course, Amelia knew exactly who her parents were, as let's just say that the supernatural side to her parentage hadn't ever been hidden from her. That being said, she also had to learn at a young age that this was a secret world she lived in, and therefore couldn't exactly go running into preschool explaining the only way she didn't miss the bell was by her father flying her there with the use of wings.

This hadn't happened yet, but I was still crossing my fingers and toes and well, anything else that would cross, for this day to happen. As come on, how cool would that be? It was like having Superman be the one to save you from detention.

Although, thinking about it, I didn't exactly think that four-year-olds got detention, and they most certainly didn't get the cane! Because let's face it, if that ever happened, then some teacher would have been forced to have the same cane surgically removed from their butt after first receiving a good thrashing from me themselves!

No one, and I mean no one touched this kid!

But I was getting off topic, and again another squirrel moment for me. My point was that Amelia knew what to keep secret, and therefore she also knew about Heaven and Hell, angels and demons and all the other supernatural lark that went with it. Neither of her parents had wanted to keep this part of themselves from her. Of course, that's not to say that this wasn't without its challenges. For example, anytime that she would spend around her mortal family, like her grandparents or her mortal auntie and uncle, Libby and Frank, things were bound to come out. Hell, even I had verbal diarrhoea and I was foolishly classed as an adult!

But having said that, the first time that this did happen, who saved the day by swooping on in there to her defence, but little old me. This was whilst we were all celebrating her third birthday and she wanted daddy to click his fingers and make the candles relight. Something he did to tease Toots, his wife, whenever she tried to blow out her own candles on birthday cakes. Which it had to be said, was ridonkulously funny!

Now, as all the adults stood around looking all awkward and shit as the kid just dropped a supernatural bomb, who was it to come to save the day but me, ruffling Little Bean's hair and saying,

"This kid, eh, just loves those Harry Potter movies!" Also, it had to be said that we had a lot to be thankful for when it came to those awesome books, as Harry Potter got blamed for a lot of stuff in front of the muggles.

"Thank you, Pipper," Dom man himself had said to me after this moment, making me wink back and say with a slap on the back,

"No problem, Dumbledore." Of course, he gave me a quizzical look in return, making me laugh and mutter,

"One day and you will totally get it, Bossman."

But in regard to saving the day from daily toddlerisms, well I was becoming a pro. Although this wasn't exactly surprising as it had to be said, I was usually quick on the mark like that. Of course, I was also usually the person putting my foot in it equally so, but I liked to think that it was all in the balance.

The natural nature of things, should we say.

Though, I had to confess that since being with Adam, he had definitely helped me stay on the straight and narrow side of the supernatural law. But it was more than just that, as he also helped me control my mad impulses and as for all the time he didn't manage it, he was there to help with the fallout of Pipisms that could have gotten me into trouble. Because, well, no one was suicidal enough to go against my belly snuggler.

"So, Uncle Adam, bust you out of prison?" I laughed at this and ruffled her hair.

"Bust you out...? Don't tell me you're turning gangster on me now, honestly your mum's going to kill me," I said, making her grin.

"Nah, Mommy loves you."

"And I love her too, Pickle Pants." She beamed up at

me and just before I could say anything more, I heard,

"And who do I love this time?" Toots asked, as she walked through the door that I had left open with a clear indication that anyone was welcome. It also had to be pointed out that she was fooling no one with that hair out of place and smudged lipstick she was trying to clean with her thumb. *Oh booyeah, Momma bear just got herself some*, I thought with a supressed giggle.

"Yeah, Toots, who you been loving this time?" I asked with an eye wag at her, one she shook her head at as she started blushing.

"Wantie Pip was just telling me the story of how she met Uncle Adam." At this, Toots raised her eyebrows at me, and said,

"That's nice, Pumpkin..." Then she paused, walking straight up to me and giving me a hug so she could whisper in my ear,

"I hope it's the watered-down version." I smirked before winking at her.

"But of course... not a tortured moment in sight," I said, and watched her face fall, straight after only realising my mistake when I heard the little voice squeak,

"Torture!" Amelia shouted, making me wince and

answer honestly back at my best friend…

"Oops… my bad."

DATE UNKNOWN…

LOCATION… *HELL*

It had to be said that, after conversing with Sophia, I had a somewhat easier punishment in mind, even if it was to be in Hell. But alas this was not to be, for everything happened pretty quickly since that day waking up in that bedroom. Quickly enough to make my head spin, for I soon found myself in front of the King once more. Although, this time I was sentenced without trial. This was pretty standard considering I had run from the bounty I'd had on my head, and in doing so painted a big guilty sign on my back.

However, what I did find surprising was that the handsome King didn't look particularly happy about issuing my sentence. In fact, if there was anything I could say to try and describe it, I would have said his gaze to be one born from disappointment. Perhaps he knew on some level this was not solely my fault. Of course, without a trial, I was left unable to defend myself and not allowed to say much other than a last statement.

Which I could think of nothing more to say than…

"My bad, Bossman."

I think I even got a lip twitch at this, as he looked mildly amused seconds before he nodded for me to proceed with him so he could deliver me to my fate himself. But this whole experience since speaking with Sophia had me viewing my life with deeper meaning. For maybe this too was fated, just like Sophia had said. Maybe there had been a reason I unconsciously ran when Pan had ratted me out… *quite literally.*

Either way, the King seemed to take no pleasure in having me cast down to Hell and with an encouraging nod from Sophia, I accepted my fate and was soon faced with another judge. One far scarier and just as handsome.

Lucifer.

The Devil himself.

Now, as for the ruler of Hell, one commonly known as the Devil and King of Kings, oh boy, but he was another royal entirely. You see the title of King of Kings was not held by many, and referred only to those who commanded kings below them. It was like being on the very top of the pyramid of power. However, unlike Dominic Draven, who held the same title, the devil seemed to be amused by my presence from the start.

At the very least I was no longer dressed like a boy, for Sophia had been kind enough to give me fresh clothing. She had even kindly allowed me to bathe for the first time in weeks, as I had started smelling sour and was in desperate need of such luxury as a warm bath. After this, I had donned a delightful forest green dress that was edged with a filigree of blue, and one that she said matched my eyes.

As for Lucifer, a known God in his own right, his vessel was one that was primarily human. Although, I knew his handsome guise could be changed with a mere thought, yet I had actually been surprised when faced with such a raw masculine beauty, for I had expected to be faced with a far more demonic presence.

But as my eyes continued that long journey upwards, for he was impossibly tall, I found myself in utter awe at the sight of such a living and terrifying legend. He looked down at me with curious eyes, before those pale aqua depths started to swirl with amusement. He had an arrogance to his manner, one only to be expected due to his position. For you could not get one higher than that of ruling an entire world and the realms within it.

A Hellish world I now found myself in.

As for his features, Lucifer had dark hair swept back from his face as if he had spent many days commanding the raging seas. This analogy was picked because he currently was dressed like the commander of the vessel. For he wore a long, black military style jacket, with swirls of metal that framed the edges in a demonic design of ancient origins. Beneath this, and in place of a waistcoat, was a bare muscular chest criss-crossed with straps of leather across his torso. Breaches enveloped strong thighs that could only barely be seen beneath the long jacket he wore. However, as for his feet and calves, these were hidden in thick boots that folded over at the tops. And in sight of such, then it had to be said that he made a strapping and deadly looking pirate.

Now, as for his disposition, Lucifer seemed in good spirits, and amused by my arrival. Of course, he wasn't the only one, as I soon saw that Sophia's father was also in attendance, and clearly had some say in deciding my punishment. A being named Asmodeus and one who looked like both siblings combined. Hence the thick black curls peppered with grey that were tied back from his face, one that looked only to be an aged version of his royal son.

Asmodeus was basically the Devil's right-hand man, everyone knew this. And as for the fruit of his loins, a pair that had proudly produced the King of Kings, who had been fated to living among mortal men... well, it had to be said that Dominic Draven hadn't looked particularly happy to see daddy dearest.

But then again, the meeting seemed to be one of mocking on Asmodeus' part. His father was known as the ruler of Lust and one of the Kings of the nine circles of Hell. It also had to be said that his realm was one of my favourites in Hell, for I always wanted to go there for obvious reasons. In truth, I had been hoping that my sentence would have landed me there, for I could have quite easily fancied myself as some naked, bound servant to the King himself. A King who was most definitely handsome enough to fall in love with, that was to be sure.

But, like I said, this was not to be.

Of course, there were many other realms in Hell, all of which had their own rulers appointed by Lucifer himself, for he was the One being. But as for the King of Lust, then like Lucifer, he too was incredibly attractive and seeing as he resembled Dominic Draven, I had to wonder if this wasn't what irritated him? Had Asmodeus purposely adopted this appearance for some nefarious reasons of his own or was it simply to vex his son?

Now, as for his choice of attire, unlike Lucifer, he had not adopted the modern-day mortal fashions but instead, was dressed like a Persian warrior with a demonic twist. No doubt another vexatious nod to his son's vessel, for the King of Kings had started out his own life claiming the body of a Persian warrior.

These were all known facts, as it wasn't just mortals that gave way to gossip about royalty. For the hidden supernatural beings of the world did exactly the same and were no different in that respect. Which was why I couldn't help but notice the smirk on Asmodeus' face when meeting with his son directly after I was delivered. One prompted by his son's own reaction, as he took one look at his father's choice of clothing, and openly gritted his teeth as if this had been a game played between them for centuries. That was when I knew that Draven's father was most likely as mischievous as I was, and someone I could class as an ally.

Well, that had been my hope at least.

As for my own King, he turned to me and placed a hand upon my shoulder before granting me my first piece of advice.

"Behave, little Imp, and endure with strength." I nodded, bowing my head in respect, biting my lip to stop myself from begging him to take me back with him.

"I...I will... my Lord," I stammered out, before he grinned and said,

"Until next time then, for I have a feeling our paths will cross again." I silently agreed, purposely making a point of not speaking for fear of what I would say. After all, I knew just as his sister did, that our paths would most certainly cross, that was if the Fates had anything to do with it.

After this, he took his leave and left me to hear what my punishment would be in what was Lucifer's imposing throne room. One that was surrounded by statues of the Kings he had appointed to rule the realms, along with Sumerian text, the language commonly used by the King of Hell.

"So, it is you who my Sarratum has mentioned in her sleep... I must say, you're not what I expected, little Imp, for you look quite breakable," Lucifer said cryptically, making me frown and question exactly what he was talking about, although in truth, I was too afraid to say much of anything.

"You are sure of this decision, my Lord?" Asmodeus asked, before it was expected of me to answer him. It was also said in a way as if my punishment had already been decided among them before my arrival. Not that I would have had much say in the matter, but it was clear between the two of them that my fate had been discussed before meeting me.

"It is decided, but I will, at the very least, allow her to get accustomed to things... I am, after all, a being of patience and understanding. Besides, if what is fated is deemed so, then surely we will have nothing to worry about and a calmer Kingdom will be bestowed upon my people once more." I opened my mouth and then closed it again when I saw Asmodeus shake his head at me, before he was the one to ask the worst question of all,

"And if he just eats her?" At this, Lucifer shrugged his shoulders as I openly gulped. Then the King of Hell simply answered,

"A pity indeed, even if undoubtably a tasty one at that... but my decision is made, now take her to the pits, for she can work in the tunnels to begin with, before their introduction."

After this, my dire situation sank like lead in my

stomach, as it had to be said that from the sounds of this conversation... it did not bode well for my immediate future. Especially not when they spoke of a beast so powerful it had obviously been causing Lucifer problems in Hell.

This was confirmed when Asmodeus said,

"Then, for all our sakes, let us hope the Fates have sent us the solution, and before the realms of Hell shake once more."

Good Gods, just what was this beast that could make even its Kings shudder in fear?

I didn't have much chance to ask before Sophia's father was leading me away, and my question as to if Asmodeus was an ally was answered when he bestowed advice upon my turbulent mind.

"Dance for him and entertain him as no other ever has before." I frowned in question.

"Dance for who?" I asked, for surely, he could not mean the beast! His knowing grin gave me answer enough. So, I allowed myself to continue to be led away from the throne room now that Lucifer had cast down his punishment and had clearly finished with me. It also seemed as if his friend had been silently tasked to deliver me to such punishment, one that gave me far more room for concern. For I was to be sentenced to the lowest parts of Hell for a whole Hellish year, which in mortal terms was about 100 years. For time worked differently in Hell, depending on which realm you found yourself situated in... or should I say, imprisoned in.

After this I questioned my fate, and this was where he explained I was to be added to some sort of workforce down there. This was no doubt thanks to a certain skill set I possessed, as just like with the rats, I was to be used to call forth creatures of a different kind, a particular Hellish worm that lived in the mountain that could reproduce at an incredible rate. In fact, had these creatures not been on the menu for the beast, then they would have had the ability to eat through the entire mountain within only half of a Hellish year.

But they clearly needed to feed the beast a lot of them for it to be sated enough to stay calm and not break free to search for its own food source. This was according to Asmodeus, who explained these details to me during our journey to the nearest portal gate.

So, this was to be my punishment. I was to farm these worms to feed some sort of demonic beast they had imprisoned down here. And this was the mighty being

Asmodeus had been expecting me to dance for.

"So, you say he will want entertainment with his meal?" I questioned, wondering if such a thing as dinner and a show would catch on in the mortal realm, missing it already.

"You will soon find out, Little One... oh trust me, of that I am certain... *and soon.*"

"And how am I to survive such a thing?"

After this, the next words out of his mouth were clearly all the warning I needed.

"By using all the talents the Gods gave you, Child..." Then he paused, and whispered down at me with a wink...

"Lustful ones."

ELEVEN

A NUMBER OF BEASTS
DATE UNKNOWN
LOCATION: SOMEWHERE BELOW THE NINTH
CIRCLE OF HELL
THE PRISON REALM.

It had to be said that as far as punishments in Hell went, then I couldn't complain too much as it was far better than being tortured. That being said, what I hadn't counted on was annoying my jailors so much that they had ended up taking matters of my punishment into their own hands.

Of course, I wasn't without blame for the incident and couldn't claim total innocence on my part. Not when I had outwardly attacked them for goading me into retaliation. Hence, when I discovered a new level of Hell, and when they had taken it upon themselves to cast a new sentence upon me.

One of the more final kind...

I was to be food for the Beast.

Now, it had to be said at this juncture, that this turned out to be a better choice. Especially when they had originally wanted to feed me to a bunch of Hellhounds they kept as angry fucking pets! Something I knew most definitely hadn't been fated. I also knew that it would have taken a whole Spanish armada to have stopped them from eating me... no amount of dancing would have saved my skinny behind from them, no matter how cute they found their food.

But once more, I was getting far ahead of myself with my 'woe is me' storytelling, as first I needed to paint a picture of events that led to my fate in becoming food. Because it started after first stepping through the portal and finding myself facing a barren wasteland. One filled with a mountain range that seemed to surround the largest of all at its centre. In fact, the moment I was grabbed from behind and taken into Asmodeus's arms, I was soon to find out exactly what it looked like from above, as he took us up into the skies.

Angry swirls of rust red clouds clashed angrily above us as he flew us both under what looked like an eternal storm. This was so he could cross the open vista of a black sand desert and get us both to the prison. Of course, the moment we were directly overhead, I could see that each of these smaller mountains connected to the largest by a series of raised tunnels. This, making it look like tree branches connected to the centre, and it didn't take a genius to know what the biggest one housed.

The Beast.

After this short flight, I was quickly handed over to my new keepers and saying goodbye to the handsome King of Lust who, like his son, bid me farewell in a similar manner,

"Remember what I said, young one, and good luck, for you will no doubt be in generous need of it. Until next time, pretty girl." He said and unlike his son, he grasped my chin and raised my face up for a kiss, one so incredible and powerful that it had the capability to render me unconscious, as seconds later, my new Hellish world went black.

The next thing I knew, I heard a clatter sound on the

bars I found upon opening my eyes, meaning only one thing…

My prison sentence had begun.

After this point, I had no other choice but to try and embrace this new chapter in my life, which included working by day and sleeping in this cell at night, one that had been carved right out of the rock face. Because that was precisely what these mountains were, cell blocks of a different kind. The whole prison was like a beehive full of both inmates, prison guards and places for demonic creatures to live. Burrows, caves and all number of crevices were found to be home to these creatures.

As for me, my new home was the largest of one of those caverns tunnelled from the biggest mountain of all, and what looked like a purposely made prison big enough for the Devil's own beast. And as for my job, well, it wasn't exactly what I would have called fun.

For one, the Mongolian death worm looked like a mortal's large intestine that was about four foot long. Fat, bulbus, and pink was the only way to describe the worms, with their only other features being a circle of teeth at one end and a long stream of shit that came out the other. It would eat other parasites that lived in the rocks and therefore created a honeycomb of burrows.

My job was to use my unique talents to get them to come out of their holes and then stab them with a pitchfork type tool the length of a broom. Then I would deposit these poor wriggling fat bastards into a large cart. Once full, another unfortunate (which is what they named inmates of the Prison realm) would come along and take the cart somewhere. Of course, it didn't take too much guessing to know what these worms were intended for and throughout my working day, I summoned hundreds of them out from their nesting burrows.

Now, if someone were to ask me how many days it was that I lived this daily existence, well in truth I had lost count. However, it was during this time that I also discovered more about the great beast we were feeding. This was thanks to whispers from other inmates that had been forced to work down here. This also meant I wasn't the only creature forced into this life and my fellow prisoners were far more deadly than I. Although, it had to be said, none were more savvy and street smart than I, which meant that I had survived quite a few narrow escapes.

Like the gang of Tsuchinokos that literally translated into 'child of hammer'. These were snake-like beings that could choose to walk on legs that split from their bodies or slither the caves as giant grey and red vipers. They had the ability to jump great distances before jumping a second time, even whilst in mid-air. They could also snake their way up vertical drops and would latch themselves onto the rock and suck out the minerals. This act of feeding caused the worms to surface because of the vibrations the Tsuchinokos created, making them a valuable workforce. Then, just before the worms could attack, they would curl up and roll away, looking like fat red wheels travelling the mountain walls.

There were also the Nuckelavees, which were a race of nasty bastards that looked like skinless horses. Now, whenever one of these vile creatures broke free from the gates of Hell, they were known to cause epidemics and droughts in the mortal realm. It was also said that a Nuckelavee's breath was thought to wilt crops and sicken livestock, although ironically breathing over the worms kept them fresh for longer.

That was the reason they worked on the carts and were in charge of delivering a full load to its destination.

This horse-like demon was from Orcadian mythology but had its origins in Norse mythology also. It had a man's torso attached to its back as if it were the one riding the red skinned beasts, although this humanoid body had no legs. Its arms, however, could reach the ground from its position on top of the equine body, with a pair of shoulders that held a neckless head. One large enough that it rolled back and forth and looked far too big for the rest of its strange body.

As for the horse part, its head had an enormous gaping mouth that expelled a shit smelling toxic vapour and clung to its skinless frame of bare flesh and quivering muscle. A single, enormous eye sat at the centre of his long face, and was like looking directly into a burning red flame.

They were dangerous creatures and would eat anything they could get hold of other than the worms, for they were like poison to them. These, I had the unfortunate task of working with, and many a time had to use my pitchfork as a weapon to defend myself, spearing one in the eye once.

Needless to say, they didn't like that and basically had it in for me ever since. But there were also those that didn't want to eat me and had loose tongues whilst they worked. Demons of all races that liked to tell horror stories to try and scare me when I was locked away in my cell at night. I should probably mention that I had yet to gaze upon the Devil's great beast myself and had so far only heard its bone shaking roars. Mighty bellows of rage that could be felt beneath your feet, for the walls would shake and crack as it echoed throughout the prison. Of course, every time I heard this thundering sound it only made me even more fearful for their stories and the intent in telling them certainly served its purpose…

I was terrified.

Of course, I wasn't the only one, not after what we had heard, for our jailors had taken great pleasure in telling us what would happen should we fall out of line. Basically, we would be the ones to replace the worms that fed the beast.

The beast that I now knew had a name…

Abaddon.

It was most certainly fitting, for this name meant destruction in Hebrew, and for good reason, for that was precisely what he was created for. You see, it was said that one of Lucifer's hobbies was creation, being jealous of the Gods which he used to sit beside.

Lucifer had always been trying to find new ways to strengthen his armies, and what better than to create a monster from the twisted and lost souls of warriors trapped in the 7th circle violence. The most heinous, most destructive, and furious souls all found in one place. A cesspool of hatred all coming together and pulled into one mighty being.

So, as for Abaddon, it had been his hope he would be one of his greatest accomplishments in the Godly art. However, this ended up backfiring on Lucifer for he created a beast so powerful Abaddon could not be contained nor could he be controlled.

Because on paper, this theory of creating something purely out of hatred might have seemed possible, but unfortunately for Lucifer, he was to learn that a being needed far more than just simple hatred to survive...

They needed a reason to want to live.

Because hatred, pain, torment, hostility, and revenge weren't emotions that were born or simply created, they were absorbed through life. *They were experienced.* It was not something that was bred, but something gained.

Which meant that the 615 creatures before Abaddon had all died, having none survived such brutal births from the river Phlegethon. They were either too weak or too strong, ripping themselves apart when the rage became too great to be contained.

In fact, it was said that the one element that they had

needed had been the very last one expected to work.

It had been something strong enough to create will of life, the very thing and essence that gave all life the will to live and survive.

It was unsurprising then, when it was Asmodeus, the King of Lust and Lucifer's right hand man, who offered a single solution.

They made the beast with...

Lust.

TWELVE

SLAP HAPPY WORMS

So, lust had been the key.

Not that I was surprised by this as I personally had to agree with the randy bastard. Randy being another word of mine that was yet to catch on, but I had the feeling the Scottish would love it, if and when they eventually got the chance to hear it of course.

But back to the King and one, it had to be said, who could kiss me any time, for that had been some powerful sexual magic he had going on there… baboom! (Again, one of mine but more of a sound, than a word).

Asmodeus had rightly suggested that lust be added,

which wasn't surprising, as after all, his realm was overflowing with souls that were there through their own lustful sins. He believed and convinced Lucifer that lust could make any creature desire to live, and to live through the rage that had consumed all others before the making of Abaddon.

So, with Lucifer in agreement, number 616 the mighty Beast was born and more importantly... *survived*. However, Lucifer wasn't celebrating for long, as it turned out Abaddon was so powerful, he could not be contained or controlled as the Devil would have liked. He was too unpredictable, and during his first battle whereupon he was released, Abaddon ended up doing just as much damage to Lucifer's own forces as to the opposing side. Thus quickly deeming him useless for war.

After this and the mayhem he had caused to many places in Hell, including even a few earthquakes upon the mortal realm, the Devil had no other option other than to carve out his very own realm, one that would house the Beast until a more permanent solution was found... a solution Lucifer was still waiting for.

Of course, one solution he could not use was death, for Hell's King of Kings soon discovered that Abaddon could not die. He could not be beaten, destroyed or in any way stopped, other than be eternally caged. A prison it is said he has no real knowledge of. Which meant that for thousands of years, he was simply to exist. And for Lucifer, Abaddon's only usable quality left to him was that of a threat made to all who dared to anger him. In essence, he became the very thing that demons had nightmares about; a place to send those that Lucifer reserved a special punishment for.

The likes of me, for example.

I had no idea why myself in particular had been deemed fated to receive such a punishment, as I knew from experience throughout my long life and histories lived through, there were far more Dark Souls worthy of taking my place, for the death on their hands far exceeded those of my own crimes.

But alas, here I was, a slave to the Beast with my only hope that I would make it through my 100 year sentence without being the next worm on a hook. A hope I was soon to realise was far too much to ask.

Although, I had to confess, I was also somewhat curious about the Beast as, call me insane, I also felt sorry for him. After all, he didn't ask to be made, to be created with such rage he was deemed uncontrollable. It also made me wonder what became of the lustful part of him. Sure, the lingering remains of these souls that had helped in creating this Beast had aided his survival, but what of his character? What of his temperament? For surely there must have been something other than just burning rage deep inside the monster.

There must have been something he wanted…

Something he desired.

Of course, I was still terrified, but naturally the curious part of me wanted to know the answers to my questions. That being said, I wasn't suicidal enough to go searching for it and wisely kept my mouth shut on the matter. However, this was me we were talking about and well, there was only so long I could go by unnoticed for good behaviour.

I was an Imp after all.

We weren't exactly known as the most well behaved of creatures, which was why I hit my limit on playing nice and compliant, because after another long day of shovelling death worms into a cart, the very last thing I wanted was for some big bastard to prod me in the ass with a big stick. And no, this was not meant in another way, like riding below the crupper. A term that meant being done from behind like a mounted dog or anal sex, for a crupper was a piece of horse-riding kit that kept the horse's tail erect... poor bastards.

As for the one that had poked my ass, and had been doing so for what must have been weeks now, he was like most of the other guards here. Known as a Haugbúi demon, which translated meant 'barrow-dweller'. They were loosely related to the Draugr, who were defined as ghosts or spirits of the dead. Ones that inhabited a corporeal body that lived close to cairns, being a manmade pile of stones that were used as landmarks. These were so they could prey on travellers using these landmarks to guide their way, travellers who soon found themselves faced with a far worse fate than being lost. Of course, the Draugr could also be found in graves or even royal palaces, often guarding treasure buried with them in their burial mound.

Both species of demons were used as guards down here, and both types were just as deadly. But whereas Draugrs looked like the living dead recently risen, the Haugbúi looked more fierce. They were at least seven feet tall, with wide muscular frames that they kept protected by lengths of hardened bark. This had been stripped from the trees that grew in the Dead Soul Forest on the banks of the river that crossed over into the Shadowland. They had been soaked in the river Styx and for good reason, for the very essence of the water was to help create the indestructible. This represented an unbreakable oath by which the Gods took vows in this very river.

These effective, yet crude looking chest plates were attached to their torsos with hammered metal that were braced around their shoulders and waists. As for their features, red weathered skin covered their bodies, with lighter patches shown on their faces. A stripe of cream skin ran along the centre of hairless heads, and the same lighter tone brushed the length of their noses and the tops of their floppy ears. These flaps of seemingly useless looking skin hung down underneath gigantic horns that curled round like a ram's.

More facial features included stone eyebrows that flared up above beady eyes, and a parallel of short stone spikes ran either side of its bald head. A low wrinkled nose that squared at the bottom by its nostrils, continually snorted as if it was trying not to sneeze, making its hollowed cheeks puff out with the effort. These over pronounced cheek bones also created shadows by the lines of its jaw, that then tapered into two smaller horns that jutted out either side of its pointed chin.

They carried with them a various collection of weaponry, being anything from large hammers to double edged blade swords, and some even held a hooked spear, like the bastard who was taunting me now.

"I wouldn't do that again if I was you," I warned in my meanest voice, one that was met with an evil and sadistic laughter as he clearly didn't take me seriously.

"Or what, huh, what are you going to do, little Imp?" he taunted, elbowing his friend as if he had told a jolly good joke. They had both been doing their rounds and found me in the caverns doing my job, and decided to try their luck at some demonic fun. I knew this when he poked me again, just as one of the worms was approaching the end of the tunnel. I gritted my teeth before releasing a sigh, and then made the foolish decision that it was time to teach these brutes a lesson. Which meant I did something that I knew was potentially going to get me in a lot of trouble and admittedly, the kind I might not be coming back from.

But you see, that was the thing about losing your temper, sometimes you did so, damning the consequences when your actions could not be contained, for the Beast was not the only one who, in that moment, was being fuelled by rage.

"What am I going to do…?"

I answered the moment the worm popped its little fang ridden head out. So I grabbed it, wrestled it under my arm before pulling it from its home. Then once I had it in my hold and it was secure enough to stay there, I gave them my answer.

"This!" I shouted, before whipping the worm around and slapping one of the guards in the face so hard, that he fell to the ground. Then, just as the one that had poked me was about to retaliate, I threw it at him, aiming for his man giblets and said,

"Here, let's give you some more girth to that pudding prick of yours!" Then, as the worm flew through the air, there was that single moment of panic that flashed in his gaze before the end of the worm with all of the teeth latched itself on to his manhood. He howled in pain, as it now looked as if he had a giant floppy penis that he was making dance side to side as he shook his hips in vain.

I couldn't help it, but I burst into laughter, pointing at it hanging in between his legs, whipping ground like crazy as it chomped its way at the guard's favourite appendage. He screamed, wildly shaking his hips faster this time and trying to get the thing off him.

Meanwhile, his friend was just coming to after being slapped with the body of blubber. As for me, I knew my time for laughter was over, so I tipped up the cart filled with the worms I had recently collected, covering the guard in them. Doing so now so he would have more trouble getting up, therefore giving me more time to escape.

Naturally, after this I ran for it, picking up my pitchfork, so I had a weapon that didn't include a wrestling worm. Thankfully, from the endless days that I had been working the tunnels, I knew my way around. So, I was hoping to make it to one of the larger caverns where I would have a better chance at hiding from my pursuers. Because I knew if I could just make it to some of the higher levels, then I would possibly have a chance of escaping this mountain. From there I could potentially bribe my way out of the prison realm, although with what exactly, I didn't know yet.

Gods, but I would have picked Tartarus over this shithole, I thought as I continued to run, ignoring the shocked looks from the other inmates. Some shook their heads as if silently calling me foolish and others looked on with wistful optimism, no doubt hoping that I would achieve my task and therefore make it achievable for them to do the same one day.

But I should have known.

No one escaped the prison realm.

Because, if an almighty Beast like Abaddon couldn't achieve such a feat, then a little Imp like me had no chance. I knew this the moment a loud siren was sounded, one that echoed through the larger caverns and travelled like wind throughout the warren of tunnels. It was at this moment that I heard the thundering feet of my prison guards, for they had sounded the alarm. One that no doubt, was rarely heard…

A prisoner had escaped.

Needless to say, after this point I didn't get far, for I turned a corner I knew led into one of the largest caverns and found myself faced with unbeatable odds, for no amount of Mongolian death worms being slapped in the face were going to get me out of this one. I knew that the moment I was grabbed from behind, and heard a snarled warning hiss down my ear,

"Looks like the Beast is eating Imp tonight!"

Then, after this, I felt a blow to the back of my head, and swiftly fell unconscious with one last random thought running through my little Imp mind...

Would I be crunchy?

THIRTEEN

FISH... HOOK... SINKER

Well, once again I found myself facing undeniably low odds at survival, because I finally discovered what happened to all of those poor unfortunate Mongolian death worms that had been sentenced to the same fate I now faced.

I had literally become the next worm on a hook for the Beast.

Because the next time I opened my eyes, was just as they were tightening a noose around my neck, getting ready to dangle me off a hook over what looked like a bottomless pit. One that was no doubt home to the notorious Beast, Abaddon.

This was when all those demonic faces started laughing at me, taunting me with what was to become of my future. Some of the lazy scobberlotchers even started to take bets on how long I would last before I was cooked alive, and Abaddon was picking his teeth with my little bones!

However, before this could happen, and seconds before they could kick me off the side, I slipped free of the rope and tried to fight my way once more to freedom. I made it through some of the crowd, impressing even myself, but this was until the big bastard I had permanently injured, both to his pride and to his now non-existent manhood, suddenly barged his way through the crowd.

"Oh, shit balls," I muttered, just before he grabbed me and literally tossed me over the side of the cliff face. I screamed as I went down, thinking this was it… I was a dead Imp for sure! Unbelievably, my last thought was a strange one as I fell, feeling somewhat disappointed that I wouldn't get at least one chance to see the Beast, that I would die without knowing what he looked like… but then again, I didn't think I was the first being to have strange last minute thoughts seconds away from death.

But alas, death did not meet me this time, as I landed

too soon to cause much damage, let alone death, despite how hard I banged my head on something. After this, I wasn't given much time to think what exactly it was I had landed on, because I could feel the blow to my head start to take hold of my consciousness again. So, aware of this, I decided on one last act of defiance before I fell completely under, I held up my hand and gave the bastards that were now laughing one last gesture goodbye,

I held up my middle finger.

Unlike the mortal world, I knew they would recognise this insult that was one commonly used down here in Hell. One that meant fuck you, and was yet to catch on with humans, but when it did, I just knew it would be a world class favourite.

I knew this because after doing so, the laughter died down and I fell unconscious with what I swear was a smile of satisfaction on my face.

***

The next time I came to couldn't have been much time later. The mountain started to shake, waking me from my nightmares and proving there were reals ones yet to face.

I knew this the moment I woke fully and found myself on top of a pile of soft squidgy dead worms. Worms that, potentially, I myself had been the one to spear to death with my pitchfork. So, this had been what I had landed on when falling. Great, just great I thought with bitterness as the saying went, 'what good came of jumping from the flame and into the fires of Hell.'

Well, I could easily answer that one…

Nothing but death, that was what!

Which made me question just how long I had until that happened, as perhaps I should myself have taken bets! Because now I could also feel a distinct movement of being lowered and it was only when I started to get my bearings that I realised why this was.

"Oh, monkey shit," I muttered as I pushed myself up from the dead worms beneath me and looked over the side of the large bucket. One that was currently being lowered down to an even deeper level of the caves. I looked back up and for the first time, I could see an entire city above me cut out into the very core of the mountain. Little lights from flames that had been lit shone from between the crevices that made doorways and glassless windows. The further down I was lowered, the smaller it all became to the point that I lifted up my hand and could now cover what I knew was colossal archways with my thumb.

Also, from where I was positioned it looked as if the very centre of the mountain was near hollow, as a great split carved its way through the middle like a gigantic, jagged pathway. It reminded me of a great river that had eroded its way through the mountain, leaving both sides left for demonic life to live in. These two sides were connected at different points where giant rock faces and cliffs were at the closest points to connect, doing so by precarious looking wooden rope bridges. I also looked to see many other buckets just like the one I was sat in being dropped down. They were the size of a carriage, and were lowered by giant mechanisms bolted into the rocks high above, ones that thick chains were being fed through. I could also see from a distance that it looked as if some of the demonic creatures that had been above to witness my demise were crawling down the chains. No doubt they didn't want to miss out on the show, or they needed to lay witness to my death so they could name the victor who won the bet.

Either way, they were wise not to come down too close and remained at a safe distance up the chain. I also now knew that this was how they fed the Beast who they obviously kept at the lowest part of the mountain. This was, no doubt, to ensure that Abaddon remained contained.

It made sense that the workforce was imprisoned above and as far from the Beast as the guards could get. For they needed to keep this huge workforce safe to create enough food so he would not be tempted to go looking for food himself, breaking free in the process. It was the only explanation that made sense, for surely Lucifer would have just left him down here otherwise, and with little care if he fed or not.

That meant one thing...

The Beast could escape if he needed to.

The echoing clunk of the chain feeding its way through the metal wheel felt like my own death knell was being wrung out as it warned me of my limited time before reaching the great pit below. There had been many whispers of this great pit, most of which had come from threats from the guards, threats that I now knew had not been empty.

I couldn't help myself as I looked over the edge to try and see what awaited me at the bottom. A slither of light from a glowing line got thicker and thicker the further down I travelled, telling me that there was a river of lava at the very bottom. I could only wish that the Beast did not like his Mongolian death worms cooked and well done before consumption took place.

Or this Pip was going to get extra crispy real soon!

Thankfully, I soon found my bucket getting closer to a balcony ledge cut into the rock, and one that could be seen easily due to the glow of the flowing magma immediately below it. I let out a relieved sigh as this ledge acted nicely as a deposit for the worms and well, now myself, as the moment we came close enough, the chain stopped, and another clunking sound could be heard. It was one that signalled something new, before only two sides of the bucket started to release the chains at the front. Then horror struck as this started tipping the large container and I panicked, trying in vain to scramble backwards in hopes of staying inside the thing. Of course, it was no use as I had little choice then but to fall forward, having nothing to grip onto. Which meant there was only one way to go for me as the slimy worms pushed me forward so I fell in a heap among them.

I quickly scrambled to my feet and jumped up to try and grab hold of the bucket ledge before the chain could start pulling it back up. However, my fingertips had only barely grazed it before the bucket was raised up enough so that I had missed my opportunity.

"Fuck... fuckery, fuck, fuck!" I swore in hopeless

desperation as I watched the last chance of my survival now growing smaller and smaller above me.

It was official…

I was doomed.

I knew that, the moment the floor beneath me started to shake and a loud growl started to echo along the walls of the mountain. But of course, the Beast knew it was feeding time, he could no doubt smell it. I decided I couldn't just lie here and wait to be scooped up by some gigantic demonic hand and shovelled into an even bigger mouth. No, my best chance was to try and hide in hopes of finding somewhere I could survive this nightmare without him even knowing I was here.

Yes, this was a good plan.

The long ledge that I found myself situated on was as wide as the streets of London, and currently filled with heaps of worms that were mounded high where the buckets had dropped their loads. I looked up to see how high the wall was before the next level, and soon realised this wasn't an option. It was at least as high as the Cheshire Cheese pub, being over two storeys up. It was also a sheer rock face that looked impossible to climb. I turned and looked the other way, to see that opposite was nothing but a sheer drop down to a flaming river that held only one destiny... *death.* A river that looked to be wider than the River Thames and from where I was positioned, completely impossible to cross.

So, as the sound of the Beast drew nearer, I feared I had little option left than to plaster myself against the wall, knowing that the only place left for the Beast to appear was from above. As I said, it was obvious he knew when feeding time was, for only minutes later I found myself wishing I could take back my earlier madness. Because what had I been thinking, regretting that I may die without first seeing the Beast?!

Well, I was certainly about to eat those thoughts... Hell, I was about to choke on them, as now, for the first time, I found myself faced with my fate.

For the Hell's only fear,

Abaddon...

Had arrived.

FOURTEEN

A BEASTIE SNACK

"*Christ in a pie!*" I uttered on a horrified whisper as I got my first glimpse of him.

He was even bigger than I'd ever imagined!

Because looking up now, I could only see a portion of his gigantic arm. Naturally attached to this was a hand, and one that was reaching over the ledge and scooping up the nearest mound of worms. His hand was such a size he could have picked up a horse, maybe even two!

As for its skin, it looked as if it had been made with the bones of its victims, as hardened flesh was cast in a reddish hue and looked even more demonic. This was thanks to the glow of the lava that cast the rocks in the same light. In truth, I was thankful for it, for this deep down into the mountain without it and I would not have been able to see my hand in front of my face, but as it stood now, I could see everything, and my only hope was that it could not see me due to the same light.

I sucked in a shuddered breath, once again cast in the shadow of its limb as it reached over and took another scoopful of the next mound of worms. This was before lifting them up into its awaiting mouth. I looked up and could see under its face as its jaw worked to chew its meal. Pieces of the worms fell from the corners of its lips and rained down either side of me. Thankfully, I had a strong constitution, strong enough not to want to vomit anyhow.

I decided to continue to shimmy along the wall, doing so unseen, as so far this had worked in my favour. I also had to hope that this ledge led somewhere, for I knew I couldn't just stay this way, as my luck was about to run out at some point. However, I didn't expect it to run out so quickly as the ledge narrowed in one part and I must have walked out too far, for the second I heard the monster roar behind me, I knew I had been seen.

"Oh, fuck it!" I said, before running towards what

looked like the largest mound of worms yet. In fact, it was so large that it formed into some sort of hill, and one that was overflowing into the lava. I found this odd, as why would he leave the biggest one untouched?

My internal question was not left unanswered for long, as it was only as he reached out to grab me that I realised why this was. It started when I heard the clang of thick chains as they were pulled taut, and I braved looking behind me. I did this just in time to see his demonic hand nearly reach me, and one that would have swallowed my body whole. He had been only a foot away from grabbing me.

"Ah!" I shouted in fear, but thankfully the Beast's fingers curled without its bounty, one that would have been my body in its grasp. Then, when it soon became clear that he could not reach me, he reacted. A roar of anger shook the mountain walls once more before a whining sound replaced it. I frowned in question before I felt safe enough to look back at Abaddon and for the first time, take in the entirety of the Beast behind me.

"Oh my, upon the Gods!" I uttered in complete awe. I had never seen a beast like him, he was... Gods, but he was incredible! In fact, I found it hard to tear my gaze from him, trying to remind myself I should be running in blinding fear. However, I wasn't doing this, no, instead I was simply staring at him in complete and utter awe!

Abaddon was the size of a building, with a huge body that would have looked even bigger had he not currently been resting on folded knees. I mean this was understandable, considering not many people stood up whilst eating and clearly the Beast was no different in that regard. He had long arms that reached the floor like an ape, and his skin was a mass of bones that lay beneath the flesh like an uncovered burial ground.

As for his head, it sat in between huge, rounded shoulders that bunched up in his anger, and he had no neck to speak of. His face was a sloped forehead and huge mouth that barely had room for the nose in between, if that was what you could call it. Twisted horns of grey bone curled up from what looked like slits for nostrils and reached up and out towards the sides.

There was little doubt that the most terrifying part on him was his mouth, as it was a mass of teeth and fangs that circled in rows down his throat. Now, as for his eyes, these were small black depths situated in open folds of his skin at the sides of his head, that looked at me now with what looked like curiosity.

In fact, it looked as if we were both taking our time looking at one another, and my gaze finally settled on the chain connected to one wrist. I frowned in question before looking at the other hand, the one that had been reaching for me, only to find that at some point he had managed to break free one of his restraints for a shackle remained with only a few links of chain attached to it. However, with the other hand, he had not been so lucky at accomplishing breaking free, and this was what had prevented him from reaching me.

Although, this obviously hadn't been through lack of trying. As even now, I could see as his eyes narrowed at me that he would try again. Something that happened a second later, and in an almost desperate attempt to try and get at me, he started to yank harder and harder at the chain. My eyes widened in fear for a moment as his efforts started making rock dust rain down from above with the force of his strength. He seemed desperate to get to me and I had to say I almost felt sorry for him. This, despite knowing what could happen should he manage his task. That given the opportunity, he would have most likely just popped me in his mouth and started chewing.

STEPHANIE HUDSON

Yet, despite this knowledge I still couldn't help but feel sad, knowing of how he came to be and what his life was now. An endless eternity chained up down here was no way to live. Not all alone. Because I felt his pain and I felt his sadness, for despite what they believed, it wasn't all rage and hatred at all. Because I could see that there was a longing in his eyes. Something, no doubt, no one else ever got close enough to see. But I could, and in doing so I could tell it was almost as if something else had been born into him. Something that had slipped through the cracks of creation and given him an unexpected aspect to his personality.

I took this quiet moment to glance up as the buckets continued to travel back to where they had come from. That's when I noticed the pissed off faces of those that had dared to travel down with them, as they would be forced to face the others knowing that I had survived. I couldn't help it, but I wanted to rub this fact in by giving them the finger once more.

Of course, just how cocky I could continue to be was anyone's guess, as I had a feeling that all depended on how long I could stay out of his grasp for.

And getting back to the Beast in question…

For long moments we continued to stare at each other, and I felt comfortable doing so now that I knew I was out of his reach. I looked behind and saw that I was right, there was an entrance beyond that led to a different part of the cave. One that could only be reached behind the biggest mound of worms. It was clear to me now that there had been a flaw in the design when lowering the last bucket onto the ledge. No one had realised that they had constantly been dumping worms that he could not reach. Of course, these worms would make a small mountain until having nowhere else to go but to constantly overflow into the lava below.

"Well, that sucks, I bet that teases you something rotten," I said, making the Beast stop suddenly what it was doing and look at me as if questioning the sound that just came out of me. Then he opened his large mouth a little and a whining sound was emitted.

"Aww, I guess you don't get much conversation down here, do you?" I said, speaking again and seeing the same reaction once more, for it was clear he was curious. Then when I didn't say anything for another few minutes, he reached down and continued to eat the mounds of worms that he could reach.

As for me, I looked at the entrance on the other side of the worms, knowing that all I had to do was climb up them and slide down the other side and I would find my exit. But for some unknown reason I didn't do this. No, instead I sat down on one of the worms and continued to watch him. In truth, he utterly fascinated me and I him, for I could see his gaze continually glancing my way. He almost looked wary, or was it worried that I may disappear. I decided to test this theory as I stood up quickly making his whole head turn my way. Then, when I started to back up, he made that same whining sound he had made when he had discovered I was out of his reach from grabbing me.

"You don't want me to leave?" I asked, receiving that same curious look and call me crazy, but I actually found it cute as he tilted his large head to one side as if trying to understand me. Of course, this was also when I discovered he did in fact have a neck, one that just grew with movement when needed.

"I guess I could stay for a little bit longer," I admitted, as to be honest he was becoming less scary to me by the second. But then again, I couldn't claim this would be the case if I happened to be in his reach once more. especially say if I was on the way to his mouth and a one stop ticket to digestion Ville.

I sat back down, and the moment I did I watched as his giant shoulders slumped as if he was relaxing. Then he continued to eat, and I continued to watch until all of the worms in his reach had been consumed, all except the ones I was sat against. Again, I couldn't help but feel bad for him, having all of these worms he couldn't reach as a temptation every day, growing until then being forced to watch as they wastefully fell into the lava below.

It was in this moment that I decided to do something about it and once again when I stood up quickly, he tensed and made a move like he was going to try and grab me again.

"Easy, big guy, I'm not going anywhere… look, I'm trying to help," I said, grabbing my first worm and throwing it towards him. However, when he didn't move to grab it, I decided to be a bit braver and quickly ran towards it. Then I kicked it further before quickly running back again to a safe distance. This made it so that it was definitely within his reach this time. He gave me a curious look again before reaching down to pick up the single worm, making it look tiny in between his fingertips. Then he lifted it, sniffed at it and then when satisfied it smelled the same as the rest, he tossed it in his mouth. After this, he nodded to the pile as if telling me silently that he wanted another.

"Again?" I said, making sure my tone was questioning and hoping he would understand. He obviously did because he nodded again, butting his head this time. So, once more, I picked up the worm and tried to toss it further so I wouldn't have to run and kick it. I had to say it was quite a lot of work as they weren't exactly light, and it was a little bit like tossing up a child sized sack of meat.

Hence, after doing this for twenty or so worms I was heaving out my breaths, and had to ignore the butt of his head telling me he wanted more.

"Okay, okay, big guy, you're going to have to wait because I'm tired," I said, finding myself slipping down to one of the worms that had tumbled when I had been moving them. However, what I didn't realise was that this had put me closer to him, and he realised it before I did, because I was just leaning over to catch my breath when suddenly looking down at my feet, a shadow fell over the top of me. In fact, for a moment I likened it to when the shining sun fell behind the clouds.

I slowly looked up as the palm of the creature was descending, and I had no time to run before I was suddenly scooped up myself in Abaddon's grasp.

And finally, for him…

I had been captured by the Beast.

FIFTEEN

BEASTIE LOVIN'

This was it.

This was the end... I was sure of it.

Although, it had to be said that when I saw that hand descending down above me, it was only part of my life that flashed before my eyes. And in truth... *it was honestly a sad and depressing sight.*

A sad and lonely existence.

I felt as though I had so much to give, yet there was never the right person who had ever been there to take it. I had so much love inside me I knew that I was a good person deep down in my heart, despite being a Shadow

Imp. But I felt as if I had never really been given the chance to express it. Not to the right person anyway, and I most certainly hadn't ever had it shown to me in return.

I felt as if my life was being cut too short because of this and in that moment, I didn't know whether I wanted to scream and beg him to let me live or just welcome death. So, as my sad little life continued to flash before my eyes, I clung on to the good times. The times that I had been happy. The times that I had made my own happiness despite being alone or with the wrong person.

That's when I realised most of all…

I wanted to live.

I wanted to live on and rectify the mistakes I had made in the past, and instead of making them over and over again, I wanted to learn from them. I wanted to do things differently this time. Of course, having this life epiphany at the very moment you faced your death no doubt happened to a lot of people. Which meant in reality, the timing really sucked donkey dick!

Though, I had to say that the thing that surprised me the most about my current situation was how surprisingly gentle he was being with me. Especially seeing as I was currently locked in the palm of his hand with his large fingers acting like a roof over my head. Because I knew that he could have quite easily crushed me with next to no effort on his side. But I knew that with how loosely his fingers were held above me that he was making a conscious effort not to kill me… not instantly anyway. Yet either way, it was still a rocky ride, and I couldn't help but hold on to the hardened skin that surrounded me, one filled with enough handholds and footholds that at the very least I could hold myself steady.

But then light soon erupted above me as his fingers peeled back and I soon found myself face to face with the creature, one that quite literally held my fate in his hand. But then suddenly he picked me up with his other hand after grasping my leg so I was now dangling upside down in the air. I had to say that the way he looked at me now, well had I not been faced with my current situation, then I would have laughed, for he looked so disappointed!

Not that I was surprised by this, as I wouldn't have exactly called me a meaty meal. And he knew it, especially when his other hand came closer, and he extended a claw tipped finger that curled around like a black talon you would have found on a bird of prey. Then, with the back of it he poked at me in the stomach, making me swing with the force, although I could tell that for him it was most likely considered gentle.

However, it was in this moment that I couldn't help myself or my reaction...

I giggled.

But what could I say, I was both extremely ticklish and potentially verging on delusional. So, I burst into uncontrollable laughter and in doing so, I totally took him off guard, as I doubt he had ever been faced with his food laughing before. It was at this point that he lowered me back to the ground, making me do a handstand as I landed that way. Then I jumped back to my feet, making him jerk back a little as if surprised.

After this, I decided I had probably pushed my luck to its limit so started to walk quickly to the side, hoping this meant he was letting me go. But then I only got so far before one of his hands came crashing down in front of me creating a wall of hardened flesh.

"Okay, not that way then," I muttered, turning to go the other way when the same thing happened again, creating another barrier with his other hand.

"Whoa!" I shouted, as the force of it made the floor shake beneath my feet. This was when I lifted my hands up in surrender and said,

"Okay, okay big guy, I get the hint!" But by this point it was no use as I had obviously done the damage. I knew this when both his hands started to move closer to me, trapping me in front of him.

"Oh no... not good... not good, Pipper," I muttered, before dropping to the floor on bent knees and covering my head with my arms as I waited for him to crush me in between his hands.

Surprisingly, *it was something he didn't do.*

No, instead, he simply scooped me back up into his hands before tipping one so I would fall into his left palm. So, I bravely stood back up as he started to bring me closer to his mouth and I convinced myself that this was it for me. It was beastie feeding time. Which was why I quickly held out my hand and shouted,

"Stop!"

Now what utterly amazed me was that he did!

He stopped.

So, taking this as a good sign and before he could change his mind, I thought of the advice that Asmodeus had given me, so I started to do something many would have deemed insane and began to dance on his palm. In truth, I wasn't sure you could even call it a dance, as I just started going through things that I had learned from the different cultures I had lived through. Either way, I spun my body around before doing a backflip and landing on my belly and hands beneath me.

Now the sight of this stunned him at first but the second I landed, he jerked back as if shocked. Then he raised his other hand and very gently with the curve of his talon he nudged me. It was as if he was testing to see if I was still alive and I quickly popped back up onto my feet, making him once again jerk his head backwards.

After this something incredible happened, as he emitted a sound that was like a deep belly rumble finishing with grunt.

"Oh wow, was that a laugh, big man?" I asked with a smile, before testing my theory that it could be. So, I did the same move, spinning my leg around before jumping and doing a backflip where I landed on my belly once more. And just like the last time I felt the nudge of his smooth black talon at my side. I grinned to myself before I jumped up again, this time holding my hands out and shouting,

"Ta da!" At this his head jerked back and like before,

he started laughing, making the same sound only deeper this time. It was even loud enough that it caused a bit of a landslide on the opposite side of the river, making me look around in shock as rock slid into the lava below. I even looked down, holding onto his hooked thumb to see his belly jiggling thanks to his hilarity.

"You know, you're kind of cute when you laugh… although clearly dangerous," I said, making him stop and tilt his head as if he was trying to understand me. So, I decided to go back to something he was understanding, which was having me entertaining him. I continued to dance and fall and spin around in his palm and he in turn relaxed back against the rock face to watch me. Every now and again after I popped back up, he would release what seemed like a contented sigh as if he was… well…

Happy.

However, it was only when I finally started to lose my breath that I slumped down as my tired legs needed a rest. I leaned back against the fingers that he kept curled up to keep me where he wanted me. It was like a fleshy cage that only had one exit and that would have been to slide down his wrist and arm. But I had to say, now knowing that he wasn't planning on eating me any time soon, it was easy to relax. So, I pulled my legs up and rested my folded arms on the top of my knees so I could catch my breath.

Something he allowed me to do.

Then, as I did this, I looked around to see a big opening off to one side that looked as if it led into a larger cave, one that was darker than being out here thanks to the river.

"It must be really boring down here all by yourself?" I asked knowing that he wouldn't answer me but instead just continued to stare at me.

"Well, at least we've got each other for company now, although all that dancing kind of made me hungry," I said, just as my belly started rumbling and the sound echoed loud enough for him to hear. Again, he jerked back slightly and then the most curious thing happened. As if he understood what this sound meant he reached down and with his long talon, he speared one of the worms. One that must have tumbled from the large mound after I had been working at it to get him some. Then, with it now impaled at the end of his claw, he lifted it to his palm and flicked it off his nail, so it rolled right in front of me.

"What's this?" I asked curiously, just to be sure I was seeing this right.

Was he trying to feed me?!

This was confirmed when he nudged it with the back of his talon, making it roll closer to me. It was almost as though he was mimicking my own actions that I had done for him. Then he nodded his head as if silently telling me to go ahead. Of course, I had never eaten one of these worms, as our rations had only ever been a bowl of soggy liver root called, kabattu, which translated as 'liver' in Sumerian. This was no doubt due to its colour and shape as it resembled the human organ.

This particular root was bitter, and was only made edible after being cooked and then soaked in water to ferment for weeks. It was unfortunately the only food we were allowed as the worms themselves were solely bred for the beast and no other. Not that they had ever looked all that appealing but then again, neither did a bowl of kabattu.

But now, well it looked as if I might be down here for a while and unless I wanted to starve, then I knew I needed to give it a go. Now what I was supposed to eat it with I didn't know as there weren't exactly any sharp implements lying around here. Which was why I lifted up my hands to show him, and then pretended to fail at gouging out the centre of the worm before telling him,

"I don't have any way of eating it." Then I opened

my mouth wide and pointed to my teeth that were pretty pathetic compared to his own.

"See, I don't have lots of fangs and sharp teeth like you." Then I started biting down as if pretending to chomp through the air before lifting up my shoulders in defeat.

Well, let's just say that after this little show, he got the message pretty quickly. I knew this when he suddenly used the tip of his razor talon and sliced through the worm twice, creating a thin slither that he speared at the end so he could hold it out to me. Then he nodded again with this flat bread sized slither hanging from his nail in front of my lips. I had to say once again, it didn't exactly look like the most appetising thing in the world, but then again, I was half starving. However, it wasn't like I had ever been picky, for I was ashamed to say I had eaten far worse in my days on Earth. Raw fish straight from their shells being one of them.

So, I shrugged my little shoulders and took a bite, and I had to say I was really surprised to find the texture was like cooked chicken, and its taste was actually sweet, like fruit. In fact, my eyes grew wider in shock, and I made yummy yum sounds after taking the slice off the tip of his nail and enjoying my unusual meal. Once I had finished the plate sized slice, he nodded again after cutting another piece, feeding me like some pet of his. I had to say it was nice to have someone care enough to want to take care of me, and I couldn't help but grin and smile and chuckle as I ate my meal.

Then, when I was done, I belched, making him tilt his head at the sound as I giggled and patted my belly. He looked as if he was about to make another slice for me, when I shook my head and patted his nail telling him,

"I'm full, you have the rest, sweet cheeks." He made a rumbling sound in his chest that reminded me of a demonic purr, as if he liked my reactions to him. After this, I belched one more time and relaxed back against his fingers that were still curled up protectively as if preventing me from falling off.

Amazingly, it was the first time in a long time that I actually felt contented.

"You know, I think that's the most full I've been in ages, we don't get fed much upstairs," I said, shaking my thumb to point upwards where he must have known the rest of the workers were. He too looked up as if he could understand me, and I was starting to believe that maybe there was some truth to this.

But then he started to twirl his finger around as if he wanted me to dance again, making me laugh.

"I can do more than dance, you know, I can even sing and whistle too," I said, putting my lips together and blowing out a tune which really startled him. Enough to bang his head against the rocks making some break away and land on him.

I suddenly shot to my feet and held out my hands telling him,

"Oh shit... I'm sorry, I didn't mean to make you do that." He shook his head and grunted as if the pain barely registered with him and for all I knew, he didn't feel it at all. Then suddenly he tensed and before I knew what was happening, his fingers curled round me once more holding me tight in his fist. Then I felt the vibrations of anger rolling through him as he started to growl.

"Whoa!" I shouted, knowing now that maybe I had been wrong about him treating me so well. I mean jeez, but he could have just been trying to fatten me up first seeing as I was so skinny. Making me now question, had I been foolish thinking that I could survive this with just a dance and a little conversation.

"Stupid, Pipper!" I shouted at myself, and I was

suddenly kicking myself for not taking the opportunity when he was relaxed to try and make a run for it. Sure, he was big and would take no effort at all in catching me, but then again, I was little and could surely use this to my advantage. After all, it wasn't always so easy to swat a fly buzzing around your head now, was it?

I heard him growl and snarl, making me shake and think that my time was numbered for he had obviously growing tired of me, and the whistling had sent him over the edge! I decided my only option was to slowly crawl out of his palm and use the bumps under his skin as footholds to cling on to. So I climbed underneath to the back of his hand and the second he raised it up, I started to climb down his wrist, before getting to his elbow so I could start running up his arm.

But then I looked back to see him open his fist to find I was no longer there, and in his anger, he fisted it. Then, with his other hand, the one I had just escaped, he slammed it into the rocks as he roared. But that's when I saw it! A creature now held in that same fist that he smashed against the mountain wall. I knew what it was,

A Tsuchinoko.

Those snake-like creatures would sometimes travel

too far down in the mountain and never be heard or seen of again. This quickly had me wondering if this had been what had sparked his anger and not my whistling at all. It was obvious now that his reaction to my whistling must have shook the Tsuchinoko loose from his burrow and Abaddon had sensed it. Had he then considered it a threat against me?

I was at his shoulder now and having no choice but to hold on to one of the bulbous parts of his head as he twisted and turned trying to look for me on the floor. He had dropped what he had considered the enemy, one now nothing more than a bloody mass that stuck to the rock wall it had been slammed into.

Then he continued to look for me and when he couldn't see me, he started to make that same whining sound he had when I had been out of his reach. I had to say the sound pulled at my heart. In fact, so much so that I released a sigh and being so close to what might have been his ear, he heard it.

I started running down his back, but it was too late, as he was quick for a beast his size. I knew this when I was suddenly grabbed in the pinch of his claws from behind. A hold on me that tugged at my dress as he grasped the fabric. In fact, I had been amazed at how gentle he was, something that couldn't have been easy considering his colossal size. But other than tightening my dress at the front, he hadn't hurt me, and not once coming in contact with my skin. No, he just ended up using the dress as a way to take hold of me so that soon I was being dangled back in front of his face. Although, I would have been surprised to find the dress made it in one piece without a tear.

Then, as guilt started to get the better of me, I shouted at him,

"You scared me!" This was said in an accusing tone, making another rumble work its way up from his chest. Then he grunted before he opened his palm to his free hand and popped me down in it once more. Now feeling the need to defend myself, I told him,

"I only ran because I thought you were going to eat me!" I said, making him whine. But then he did something curious as he looked down at the creature that he had killed, and then shook his head as if he was trying to tell me the reason he got angry. That was when I realised that perhaps he could understand me, but just didn't know how to communicate back other than with slight gestures.

"Do you know what I'm saying... do you understand

me?" I asked, making him whine again in a higher pitch this time.

"Okay, so how about this… if you understand me, jerk your thumb." I then looked to his thumb and was amazed to see when he jerked it forward and then back. In fact, I was so happy that I jumped up and down and started clapping.

"Brilliant!" I shouted, making him look at me curiously again.

"You did good!" I praised, and this time when he whined a kind of clicking sound came after it.

"Did you like it when I danced for you, jerk your thumb again if yes." Again, he jerked his thumb, and I became ridiculously happy at the sight.

"Okay, okay now this is great! But before I get too carried away, let's try another question," I said, tapping my lips as I thought what it should be. Then I clicked my fingers as it came to me and said,

"Alright, I have it… okay, so let's make a jerk of your thumb a yes and we will make a jerk of your little finger a no… got it?" Again, he jerked his thumb making me grin.

"Good boy," I praised, as if he was some gigantic mutant pet of mine.

"Were you angry because of the creature and worried

it could hurt me?" I asked, making him jerk his thumb but just so I knew he wasn't doing this out of habit, I asked a question that I thought he would most likely say no to.

"And how about when I ran from you, did you like that?" His answer was as suspected, as he jerked his little finger.

"Aww... okay... well, I'm sorry for running. I just want you to promise me something, and if you do then I won't run anymore... can you do that?" Another thumb jerk told me that he could.

"No more scaring me, okay, and definitely no eating me... do you understand?" I stood back, giving his thumb more room to jerk up and down being thankful when it did.

"Good, then I think we have an understanding you and I. And I will be your friend and stay with you, and in return the rules are simple... you still understanding me so far?" A thumb jerk confirmed that he did.

"Okay, so no eating me, no squashing me, no scaring me, which includes no roaring at me, and no pushing me over... gentle, yes?" It was at this point that he jerked his thumb doing so a few times so that I would understand he was answering yes to every one of my terms.

"Good, that's good then... actually it's great!" I said,

thinking that it really was, because not only had it made my life a lot easier, no longer having to shovel worms day in, day out, the best part about it was…

I had made a friend.

"In that case, it's nice to meet you… this is the part where you give me your claw." He did this by holding it out to me, and I grabbed hold of it with both hands and gave it a shake, telling him,

"This is a greeting they do topside in the mortal realm. Now I know your name is Abaddon, and I'm Pipper, but I call myself Pip for short. Not that you can say the name, but I just wanted you to know." He jerked his thumb again, and I beamed up at him before adding,

"I'm sure we'll figure out something, some sort of way, so I know you're telling me something, maybe jerking your head or something… can you whistle… no, that's a silly question," I said, when suddenly he did something that blew me away, as he circled his chest with a finger and placed his hand over his heart.

I didn't know in that moment whether this was him trying to tell me something else, but much later I would realise it wasn't.

It meant me.

Because from that moment on, this was how he would communicate with me whenever saying my name. And looking back at it, I think it was in that moment that I first started to see myself as more than just his friend…

Because I knew deep down this was the moment that…

I started to fall in love with him.

STEPHANIE HUDSON

SIXTEEN

IMP AND THE BEAST
PRESENT DAY

"Aww, that's so romantic!" Amelia shouted, wrapping her arms around herself, and swaying before telling me,

"It's like Beauty and the Beast, and you can be Belle." I couldn't help but grin down at her. We had just finished painting my love note on the wall and were now in my bathroom cleaning the brushes. Although, it had to be said, I was the kid in this moment for I just wanted to chuck them in the bin. But no, it had been Amelia who had said we care for our planet and recycle, so no throwing good stuff away, Wantie Pip, had been her exact words. I had to say as far as kids go, this one was the bomb and the coolest of the cool!

Of course, her intelligence was always astounding people, along with her extensive vocabulary. Now, of course, I wasn't a total clueless childminder, as I had managed to tell this recap of my life as a Little Bean friendly version, even putting a cute spin on the parts that weren't well… cute.

Now, as with most things, Amelia was eating up every word like it was candy, and as we helped clean the smudges off each other's faces, she asked me,

"Did you love him?" I grinned and felt that same tug pulling at my heart that had the very first day when seeing him pat his heart when referring to me. So, as I stood up from where I had been knelt down at Amelia's level, I looked at myself in the mirror, finding tears ready to fall from forest green depths. Then I swallowed hard, holding back the emotion before telling her,

"Yes, I fell in love with him." At this she grinned before reaching up for my hand and giving it a squeeze in comfort, before telling me,

"It's okay, Wantie Pip, even the Beast gets mad at Belle

sometimes, but he always saves her. Maybe you should go find some wolves so Uncle Adam can come and save you." I laughed at this before giving her a tickle and saying,

"When did you get so smart, kiddily winkle?" She giggled again before shrugging her shoulders and telling me,

"I was just born this way." My grin grew bigger as I answered,

"That you were, kid... that you were."

After this we continued to clean our brushes in what had to be the best bathroom in the house... because naturally... *it was mine.* As for the design, well even I had to admit I had outdone myself with this one!

For starters, I had the floor painted in such a way I made it look as if it was falling away at the centre into a never-ending abyss with floating steppingstones that looked like Tetris pieces. It always made me giggle when Amelia stepped inside it as she would tap her little foot on the floor as if to make sure first it was actually still there. I would then pretend to fall in, and she would always reach out to try and grab me. Sometimes I would take her hand and fall backwards so she would land on top of me when we would burst into a fit of giggles like a couple of kids which, most of the time, we both were.

As for the toilet, the back of it looked like an aquarium but instead of having fish inside it (because hello, cruel much) it had a little figure of SpongeBob SquarePants inside. This was so that every time you flushed the toilet the water would drain away and his little arms would rise, and his face would change to one of panic.

In fact, when I first had this installed, Amelia stood there for a full hour continuously flushing the toilet and giggling to herself. At the time I had been stood by the doorway munching on potato chips and when Toots arrived to find out where her daughter was, we both continued to watch her for another twenty minutes. I had even shared my bag of snacks with her as we both found it the most adorable thing we had ever seen.

She had been two at the time.

But back to the bathroom, I also had a giant shark's head on the wall that acted as a men's urinal, that every time it felt pee pee hit its tongue, the jaws theme song from the movie would play. There was also the toilet roll holder that popped out of the wall and handed it to you when you pressed the button. I even recorded my own voice to sound like some posh version of Jeeves, saying,

"To wipe the royal butt, my lady." Something I didn't think Adam appreciated, but it was funny when he first found it and shook his head as if he didn't know what to do. Then again, I rarely ever gave him time alone to do his business and would usually ask him questions on how large his accomplishment was through the closed door. Needless to say, this was one aspect of our relationship he most likely would have picked to change, seeing as he would walk out and say,

"Last time, my Winnie."

Of course, I had lost count just how many 'last time' warnings I'd had so far.

"So, what happened after that?" Amelia asked, bringing me back to our conversation, and not long after I had just finished describing to her how I discovered Abaddon could understand me.

"Well, to make a very, very, very, very long story short, I spent years with him."

"You did?!" she asked shocked as, well, to kids, then years seemed like an eternally long time, as they usually gauged the days, weeks and months by birthdays and how long it was until Christmas.

"Yes, you see I discovered it wasn't so bad and once

I'd gotten over the fact that he wasn't going to eat me, we became friends and then he started to take care of me, and I started to take care of him back."

"And then you fell in love," Little Bean said with a big sigh that made me sigh also, both of which were done in a starry-eyed way.

"Yep, in fact, don't tell him I said this, but I think I fell in love with him that first day, after he sliced a piece of that Mongolian death worm for me," I admitted with a wink.

"Like how Uncle Adam shares his pie or his cookies with you. I want to fall in love with a boy like that," she said in a dreamy way, making me laugh. Then I ruffled her hair before straightening her pigtails and told her,

"I'm sure you will, pickle pants, in fact... *I'm almost certain of it,*" I said, whispering this last part like it was a secret... which I guess it was, as I wasn't stupid, for I knew who it was that she was destined for.

"You think he'll share his pie or his cookies with me?" she asked innocently, which made me grin as she painted a funny picture she had no clue about.

"Oh, heck yeah... actually, I think he would even share his candy with you," I told her behind my hand as if it was the biggest secret of all.

"Wow, now that would be a keeper," she said, making me burst out laughing as it was clear she had heard certain sayings from all the adults she lived with, and well, it was obvious that we were all rubbing off on her.

"Come on, we'd better get you to the dinner table, before your parents start wondering if this floor has turned into a real Tetris game and we are now falling down into the abyss of THE NEVER ENDING GAME PLAYING WORLD OF FUN!" I said, making my voice very dramatic at the end and this time making her burst out into an uncontrollable fit of giggles.

A sound that could be heard along the hallways as we exited the bathroom. But as we walked back into my personal space, I couldn't help but look longingly at the new artwork we had created, now wondering what Adam would think of it. But more importantly,

Wondering where my husband was now?

In fact, I was starting to worry, as Adam rarely could stay mad at me for long. In that sense he was very similar to his demon, as there was another part of him that couldn't stay mad at me for long either.

My Beast.

DATE UNKNOWN.
LOCATION...
NEW HOME IN HELL.

It turned out that Abaddon had indeed decided that his way of calling my name was to tap his hand over his heart. Of course, this also became a way of telling me what he wanted me to do. For example, he would pat his heart and shake his head at me if he didn't want me to do something, or he'd pat his heart and twirl one of his fingers around if he wanted me to dance for him. But either way, the sign of him patting his heart became my name to him, and I would be lying if I said that it didn't affect my own heart every time I saw it. Because in time I started to do the same when saying his name, telling him what it meant to me. Now, the first time I did this, I would never forget his reaction as he rumbled out a purr. One that came from his chest and became a sound that was reserved for when he was at his happiest.

Of course, this didn't mean we were without our little hiccups. The first of which came when he learned a valuable lesson of knowing his own strength against me. This was after I had been dancing for him and instead of trying to ask me to do it again, he flicked me with his nail to get me into action once more. However, he did it too hard and ended up flinging me across the damn cave!

It went without saying that I had not been impressed, and boy did he know it as I sulked for about a week, nursing my sore bones and bruises. But like I said, he learned his lesson and after that day, he paid special care when handling me. Plus, he whined for the entire time and didn't stop surrounding me in worms as was his way of apologising. I knew this when he motioned with his thumb after I asked him if he was sorry.

There was a lot of sorry thumb jerks that week.

But after this day, my time in Hell didn't just get easier, it became the only place I wanted to be and, that was simply because I was with him. I knew that to a lot of people it would seem strange to fall in love with such a monstrous beast, but to me, he was my monstrous beast and that was that.

We soon settled into a routine, and I would start every day the same, after spending the night snuggled up to him in the safety of his hand. One where his fingers would curl around me gently like a cocoon of warmth. In fact, I had never felt so safe in all my life, and let's just say it had been a long, long, long, lonely life. But it was more than that, for I had never felt so treasured, nor so loved. We relied on each other, and yes, the conversation at times may have been a little one sided but that didn't mean he wasn't being taught to communicate. We had our yes and no system with this thumb and his finger, but he also communicated with head nods and different sounds that I had started to learn quickly what they all meant.

As for my whistling, that no longer scared him. I also soon realised that he would get fed twice a day, so this kept me busy, as I would spend my time cleaning up after him. I also managed to break down the biggest mound of worms, giving him a little extra each day. In fact, it was on this particular day that I had finally managed to clear the last of them that I discovered the exit at the end.

It was as if it was calling to me, beckoning me to discover what was in there. Of course, I didn't want to leave Abaddon, but Imps were of a curious nature and granted, quite often it was our biggest failure. It certainly was the thing that got us into the most trouble, although my mouth could often be the cause of that.

But this curiosity also meant that every time I got closer towards it, a hand would slam down right in front of me, creating a wall of flesh as my beast warned me not to go too far. It became quite clear, and quickly, that Abaddon didn't like me out of his sight, nor did he like me too far away from him and out of his reach.

So, I wasn't surprised when I looked back at him and found him shaking his head at me, as this had been one of the first things I had tried to teach him. We still had the finger and thumb routine, but to this he had also added motions with his head by copying my own.

"I wasn't going to leave, I just wanted to look and see where it led to, that's all, I promise," I told him, patting my chest to tell him I still cared for him. But again, he shook his head at me before grasping my dress and tugging me back to where he wanted me, pointing to the spot I wasn't to pass after letting me go.

I ended up nodding with a sigh, knowing he wouldn't let me go exploring any time soon. Now, as for where we lived, I discovered that there was a large cave behind him which was more of his home. I knew this because there was a kind of nest he had made for himself out of entwined roots he had pulled from the rocks. There were also smaller tunnels that I soon discovered was where he went to do his monster business. But then he surprised me as he was actually very clean about it as he even had the intelligence to move a giant boulder in front of it, so the smell would not travel past that point.

This I appreciated as let's just say that the cavern he used as a bedpan only got flushed out with lava once a week, for I had counted the days and knew by the stench when we were close.

Fortunately, it was also in this main cave, away from the feeding platform or his shit cave, that I found water. A never-ending supply, thankfully, otherwise my time here would have been even shorter.

This water supply came in the form of what looked to be a series of small lagoons that emitted a blue glow from the bottom. The first pool was closest to the ground and was the hottest because of it. But then the next level that stepped up from the first was slightly cooler, being warm enough to bathe in. Although, the only one that was best to drink from was the one at the very top, and closest to the trickling waterfall that came through a large crack in the rock and spilled over a ledge.

Each tasted different to drink as the one closest to the ground was salty like drinking sea water. However, like I said, the top one was the best, and I knew this when

Abaddon scooped his large hand in and drank some of it himself as if showing me it was okay.

All in all, I may have had one dress as my only personal item, but at least there was a place I could wash it, along with myself, because in truth, it really made you realise what was important in life. As here I was with very little, and yet I was the happiest I had ever been. I was safe, I was warm, and I wasn't hungry or thirsty. I was also clean and most of all, I had good company. There really was very little else that I needed.

My new friend was someone who didn't mean me harm or wish me ill will, and most importantly he didn't want to use me for his own gains. I knew this when there were the times that I was too tired to even dance or sing for him, but he never got mad with me when I told him no. He would just slump his shoulders and huff in disappointment, but that was it.

Honestly, *he was the bestest friend I'd ever had.*

But then, after what could have been months, like I said that bite of curiosity got too much for me one night. And well, knowing how he would react, I waited until he had fallen asleep to discover exactly where that cave led to. So, foolish or not, I snuck out of his hand and ever so gently so as not to wake him, I climbed down from his huge body. Then I tip-toed my way out of our home and back to where the ledge was. Then I started to climb down knowing now the best way to do this, as there was a part of the rockface that wasn't as steep as when I first faced it.

Then, once I was at the feeding level, I made my way to the tunnel's entrance, leaving my monster behind for what I knew would only be a moment.

However, this turned out to be a mistake and another…

Pip Bad.

SEVENTEEN

CHAOS AND KISSING

A fter I made this stupid decision to go looking into the caves, it became the day that things changed for our friendship. Which started quickly after he woke, and no doubt was the very second he realised I was gone. And oh boy, did I hear about it! Because I hadn't been travelling through the tunnel long before discovering a locked door at the very end. I realised then that this was obviously the only access into this part of Abaddon's prison, hence the reason it was locked.

Not that anyone would volunteer to come down here unless their only intention was suicide, but it did make me wonder who exactly did have access to that door. Of course, the moment the walls started shaking and parts of the ceiling started to float down all around me, was when I knew I had to get back... and quickly at that. So, I ran as fast as I could, hoping that the tunnel didn't cave in on me and the moment I made it to the other side, I could see the utter rage and torment being unleashed.

This was when I started to really understand the full extent of exactly how much I meant to Abaddon. That he really cared for me, and it was heart breaking to witness what I had done to him by leaving, if only for a moment, for he clearly thought that he had lost me for good and the result of this was utter...

Devastation and Destruction.

Because the problem was that he started destroying things around him, and when the chain on his arm finally snapped easily as if it had been made from paper, I knew then there was no containing the Beast.

Not when true rage took over.

As now he was free he looked up, as if ready to break out completely and start climbing the inside of the mountain to go in search of me. This made me realise one crucial factor...

Abaddon wasn't a prisoner after all.

No, for he just considered this place his home. He could have broken out at any time had he wanted to. And now, it seemed the angrier and more furious he got, the more powerful he became. He even managed to grow in size, and I slapped my hands over my mouth and muttered into my own quivering flesh,

"Oh no... *what have I done!?*"

Quickly after this, I started waving my arms and shouting trying to get his attention, but it was no good... *he was too far gone.* I didn't know whether it was because I was too far away or he was too deep in his rage to notice me, but either way I knew I had to do something about it. And this time I knew it was going to take far more than just a dance!

So, I climbed back up the wall using the jagged parts that I knew I could grip onto now that I knew the place well enough. Then I raced over to him, having to be careful of his stamping feet as he literally tore a piece off the mountain and threw it into the lava in his anger. I had to duck behind him as the flaming river splurged up, shielding myself so that I wouldn't get hit by the molten spray of fire. Of course, it hit him, and nothing happened for his skin was too hardened to be affected by it.

Nothing was strong enough to hurt him... *nothing but my leaving him.*

"Oh no, come on, baby, come back to me!" I shouted with tears of guilt rolling down my face. But as I looked in between his legs, I knew then that there may be a way to calm him down. Or at the very least a way for him to know I was back. So, it was at this point that I decided to take a chance on something else. Something that was admittedly taking our relationship to a whole different level.

You see, I wasn't completely innocent enough to say that I hadn't noticed his massive, gigantic manhood that usually hung freely between his legs. Nor had I failed to notice how it had become erect whenever he saw me getting naked before bathing.

In fact, the very first time I took my clothes off, I ended up screaming out in shock as he picked me up so that he could raise me closer to his face. Once there he very gently used the back of one of his talons to examine all of me, pushing up my breasts and nudging at my backside as if trying to discover all my squidgy Pip bits.

I have to mention at this juncture, that it shamefully aroused me more than ever before and enough so that when he finally put me down to let me bathe, I had to let my own fingers roam. Then, knowing that I was still under his watchful eyes, I rubbed that special place in between my legs and made myself scream with pleasure, doing so loud enough that it echoed throughout our home in the caves and when he too roared, I looked wide eyed at him in shock, for there, in his fist, was his enormous cock spilling its seed onto the floor, and it was enough that it could have filled one of the buckets used to deposit the worms.

However, since then we hadn't taken it any further than this point of touching ourselves in front of each other. One thing was clear though, he certainly liked it when I was naked. I knew that when I woke up once to find that my skirt had ridden up to my waist and he was running the back of one finger down my legs. Of course, one of his fingers was bigger than me, so it wasn't as if he could touch me in a subtle way. Meaning I would have had to have been unconscious not to have felt it. Yet despite this, I lay still with one eye cracked open slightly as I continued to watch him stroke me as gently as he could. I knew then that something was happening between us and call me crazy, as most people would, it was becoming a lot more than just friendship.

A lot more than just loving a friend.

So, thinking back to his reaction every time when seeing me naked I decided to try my luck and hoped that this would be enough to get him to calm down. So, I quickly slipped off my dress, yanking at the ties of my bodice before letting my slip of an under garment fall to the floor. Then, as I stood before him as naked as the day my vessel was born, I started waving my arms around shouting up at him. But when I knew he couldn't hear me, that's when I decided to try my luck at touching him so, as he continued to try and destroy the place, I did my best to try and climb up his leg, and I had to say this wasn't exactly easy. It was like trying to climb a damn mountain during an earthquake!

Thankfully, and with some luck, as he panted through his rage he fell backwards, now sitting down and giving me the opportunity to get to my destination quicker. This destination of course being...

His giant penis.

Now, if I thought his fingers were big, his male member would, for many, be classed as the stuff of nightmares or for others that were crazy like me... *the stuff of dreams.* Either way, right now I was just hoping it would be a solution to get him to calm down.

At the very least I was thankful that he was not aroused for it meant I had some small hope of trying to climb the thing! Because all I needed to do was to add enough stimulation for him to feel it and stop what he was doing to see what it was, before he brought down the rock face above us which was what he was currently about to take his anger out on.

I had to say, the moment I came into contact with it, I felt like a monkey climbing a damn tree! His girth was massive, but still I was able to latch on enough that it was like trying to give a tree a hand job. Alas, I threw my body up and down whilst holding on, trying to replicate what he could do with his own hand. Then, as it started to rise slightly, I clung on as I was tipped upside down.

"Ah!" I cried out as my hair fell down past my head and became a curtain all around me. I tried to blow it out of my face before sliding down to his large sack.

"Whoa!" I shouted, just being able to stop myself before falling to the floor and when I felt confident, I swung my legs down and twisted my body around, so I was now facing the right way again. After this, I tried to climb his now aroused cock and getting so far as to reach the bulbous head at the top, one that was smooth and as big as the church bell!

Then, as soon as I saw the slit that his seed would come spilling out of, I placed my whole hand on top of it and started rubbing at the softer skin, doing so now after remembering this being a particular place most of the male population enjoyed a tongue paying special attention to. I knew I was winning when I saw a large drip of pre-release rise, one that could have filled the biggest tankard the Cheshire Cheese had!

"Gods, this is going to be a lot of cum, Pipper," I said, panting with the effort it took trying to move my whole body up and down him in an effort to pull down the foreskin. But then it wasn't surprising that this would be a lot of work and far more than regular sex. But then again, it worked as I soon achieved my goal, for the moment he felt my hand in this particular area spreading his precum, he stopped what he was doing. Then he let out a deep, aroused groan before suddenly I felt myself moving as his cock started to grow and rise up even further.

Then he looked down as I looked up and it didn't take long after he saw me to feel the pulsating beneath the flesh, telling me he was soon going to cum. Needless to say, I didn't make it out of there in time, and soon discovered my biggest flaw in this plan.

This, unfortunately, I realised too late as I was shot across the cave as if from one of the Queen's navy cannons! However, instead of a cannonball being the force that threw me forward, it was a long jet of demonic cum, one that plastered me to the wall and helped keep me there, suspended like glue.

I released a sigh after first spluttering and coughing with a face full of it, unable to help getting some in my mouth. Although, it had to be said that I was pleasantly surprised by the sweet, salty taste. Um… perhaps it was all those worms? Yep, that must have been it! Either way, I was absolutely covered in the stuff and the moment I started to slide down, I said,

"A little help here," at which my new bed partner thankfully came to my aid. He caught me in between his pinched claws and pulled me from the wall. Then he brought me closer to his face and sniffed at me, before turning around and walking back towards the water source, obviously getting the hint pretty quickly.

Once by the edge, he promptly dipped me into one of the lagoons and gave me a little swirl around before lifting me back out of the water. Once again, I was spluttering and coughing as he deposited me back on his palm where he liked me to be. After this he patted his chest and nodded over to where I had left and shook his head, which was a clear indication to tell me not to leave ever again.

"I wasn't going to leave you, I just went for a walk, and I was going to come back." At this he grunted as if he didn't believe me.

"Okay look, we have to get something clear right now... you ready for this, big guy?" He huffed but I said it anyway.

"If you ever find me not here and after a while I don't come back, it means someone has taken me. It means that I didn't leave of my own free will. Do you understand?" I asked, making him grunt at me before jerking his head and this time I knew it was done because he was still upset with me.

"I promise, Abaddon, I promise I wasn't going to leave you, why would I, I love it here." At this he scoffed again, making me release a deep sigh.

"Alright look, I went into that cave to see if there was a way that other people could get in. I'm an Imp, I was curious, that's what we do... so do we understand each other, next time I'll let you know if I want to go looking for something?" At this he shook his head telling me there wouldn't be a next time, that much was clear,

"Okay, no next time but trust me, if I'm gone again it means someone took me. I don't want to leave you... *not ever.*" At this he tilted his head as if what I had said finally meant something, then I released another sigh and told him the truth.

"And I don't want to leave you because... well, because you're the best thing that's ever happened to me. You're the first person, the first being, creature, beast, demon, you name it... you're the first one that's ever really cared for me, and you do care for me... don't you?" At this he nodded and jerked his thumb, making me beam up at him.

"I care for you too, in fact, I care for you so much that... that... *I love you, Abaddon.*" At this he jerked his head back, before he quickly jerked his thumb up and down very quickly and then he slapped his hand to his heart before pointing at it, and then pointing a finger at me. He had never done this before and I had to say there was no mistaking what it meant...

He loved me too.

"Oh, Abaddon!" I shouted his name and then told him,

"Bring me closer, I want to hug you!" I said, and he obliged bringing me closer to his face. Then, once there, in front of his eye, I pointed to my heart and then pointed to him, before I threw myself against his cheek and used a foothold on his lip, in between two of his teeth, so that I could get close enough.

Then I peppered a small area of his skin with my lips, making him rumble out a purr that said only one thing…

My beast loved me.

EIGHTEEN

ANOTHER BEAST ARRIVES

After this point our relationship totally changed. The big guy actually learned how to be somewhat affectionate towards me, and I had become incredibly affectionate towards him. I would rain down little kisses on him wherever and whenever I could, making him purr, grunt, or whine in a way that I knew he enjoyed it. He would also treat me as if I was made of glass, as if he was careful in case he broke me. He had certainly learned his lesson after the first time he had knocked me across the cave shortly after I arrived and thankfully, he had never accidently done so again.

As for our daily life, days turned into weeks, and weeks into months, then years into decades as we settled into our happy ways, and after I had disappeared for a short time this way of life also now included one of a sexual nature. Of course, this was most definitely not without its challenges. For example, since that first time I had aided him in firing his load, he and I had both learned our lesson. Which meant moving me out of the way before spilling his release and no longer shooting me across the cave with his super sperm.

But then, he hadn't been the only one to receive this sexual attention. Because he soon learned quickly from watching me how he too could aid me in finding my own release so, other than never having the feel of his cock inside me, which let's face it, would have instantly killed me and split me in two, we had, should I say…

Got very creative.

Meaning I had done everything from ride the back of his claw, rubbing myself along its ridges until screaming my release to doing the same on the top of his cock. However, because this particular act aroused him so much, he had to be extra careful. As seconds after coming myself, he too would follow me, something that would have shot me up into the air like a hot spring geyser!

However, my most favourites were the times that he would lay me down on his palm and bring me closer to his mouth where his incredibly long tongue would reach out and lick me, drenching half my body in the process. It was an act that he seemed to enjoy just as much as I did, as he clearly enjoyed the taste of me because he did this as often as he could. I always knew when he wanted a taste, for he would give me a little push at my breasts with the back of his claw and raise me up, before using the horns either side of his nostrils to pry my legs apart. Then he would open his mouth and that long tongue of his would snake out. It was one that was thinner at the end, being about the width of my leg and narrowing to the size of my fist at the tip. This was the part he used to bring me the most pleasure, both when entering my core and fucking me with it like a large cock, licking me until I was a squirming mess in his hand. I would always come screaming his name, and he would always make a rumbling sound as if he enjoyed this part the most.

This basically was our unconventional sex life, which I had to say, I had no complaints over. I also knew that whenever something enraged him, I knew exactly what to do to calm him, for on rare occasions, the guards would try and infiltrate our sacred space by clinging on to the chains that were lowered down during feeding time. I also got the feeling this was done to check to see if I was still alive or not.

Not because they gave a shit of course, but at the very least, someone wanted to know. An answer to this became apparent quite quickly, one that told them that I was not only alive, but I was actually enjoying my imprisonment. Enjoying life with the Beast, for they would find me cooing over him and trying to calm his anger. Especially when he would rip off chunks of the mountain and try to throw the boulders at them. Sometimes he would hit one and they would drop like dead flies into the lava below. Of course, I would cheer for my Beast, making him grunt and nod his head at me as if proud that he had saved me from being taken from him. Because since that day I went missing, he had taken great care into not allowing anything to happen to me, as he took my words seriously enough to know that if I ever did go missing, it would not be by my own choice.

Clearly someone wanted to know about us, as they kept their spies on us for years, and well, I had a feeling I knew who. In fact, it was about sixty Earth years later and a little over half my prison sentence when the next problem arose.

And this time… it was a big one!

Big enough that it would let all know exactly what happened if I was taken from him, as that was precisely what happened this particular night. One where I found myself gagged, tied up and being dragged away from my sleeping Beast. I didn't know what they were trying to achieve, but it soon became apparent that it wasn't the reaction they had been expecting.

Because, just as they were trying to smuggle me out of the prison, Abaddon woke up and all of Hell shook once more. Seconds after my baby opened his eyes to find me gone, he took my words and my promise to heart as he knew then I wasn't to blame. And well, even for Abaddon, it didn't take a genius as to who it was, for only a few days before this there had been more and more attempts by the guards travelling down with the buckets to assess the situation between us. Abaddon had got so mad, he had managed to kill most of them which meant the few of them that got back up to the surface, could obviously start forming a plan.

However, it was a plan that went *terribly wrong*.

This was because his rage was unlike anything that

had ever been seen before! To the point that he ended up bursting through his part of the cave and into the very next mountain. His rage only lasted a single day but it was long enough to destroy three of the mountains that surrounded the biggest one we called home. This was aided by his increase in power as he grew to an incredible size, and big enough to tear off the tops of them with his hands.

He was unstoppable… well, *almost.*

Because eventually I was pushed back into one of the carts and lowered down back to our home. However, by this point, the damage had been done, and my only hope in getting him back was to chase him through the destruction and scream as loud as I possibly could, and to a place where I knew the echo would travel to his ears. Then I sat down and waited, crying out his name as tears rained down from my eyes.

His pain at losing me was one I couldn't stand, and I hoped now that who whoever had ordered me be taken from him had learned their lesson. Of course, it was to be almost twenty years later that I was to discover the answer to this. For they hadn't learnt their lesson at all.

Not. One. Little. Bit.

This became apparent after one night when I heard my

name being whispered like some spell was being cast. It was strange, as though I knew what I was doing was wrong, but I felt compelled to do it all the same. I knew the Beast inside and out by now, which also meant I knew when he was down for the deep sleep, something that would happen once a week. It was also something I gathered the people that took me the first time knew as well.

First, his fingers would always loosen their hold on me, and second, his breathing became heavier, always making it a cooler night for me as it was like sleeping in the wind.

However, this particular night, my mind was forced to tighten up my dress and leave his outstretched hand to go in search of what was making the sound. So, in a sort of dazed state of mine, I made my way through our cave to where I had done that first time I had been curious enough to see where the tunnel had led.

I climbed down the wall and as I entered the tunnel, I saw for the first time that the door at the end was open. I looked back, knowing that something didn't feel right and was just about to leave to go back to Abaddon, when suddenly I was grabbed from behind.

"Ssshh now, little Imp, or he will wake, for the hold on his mind will only last so long." A voice spoke in my ear, and I instantly knew who it belonged to for he wasn't a Being you ever forgot.

"Llluc…ifffeeer," I whispered against his hand in shock now I was fully free of my trance.

"Wwwha do… waant?" I asked in a fearful, muffled tone.

"Easy now, for I only wish for the chance to speak with you and nothing more… now, if I let you go are you going to scream, or are you going to play nicely with me, little Imp?" I murmured again into his hand, and he could guess that I told him it depended on what he had to say.

"I have a proposition for you I wish to discuss, and then I will leave, you have my word." This time I nodded, and he peeled back his fingers from where he had covered my mouth. I turned around to face him to find he had pulled me back into a room. One I knew Lucifer himself had created for the purpose of this meeting, as there would have been no reason for such lavish furnishings to grace this place. Like the throne style chairs, with their overly high backs carved from dark wood and deep red cushions draped in silk. Hand woven rugs from the Far East covered the floor, adding colour to the bare rock walls that held nothing but curled iron torches that were lit with a blazing flame.

Lucifer held out his arm towards a seating area, acting like a gentleman, one I most certainly didn't know he could be, then he said,

"If you will grace me with your time, little Imp." I nodded, thinking it wasn't really wise for me to deny him such a request. Especially seeing as he could simply have snapped my neck in seconds. Although, how Abaddon would have felt when waking up and finding me dead and broken was a nightmare that all of Hell would have woken up to as well, because let's just say I didn't think it would end well for the Devil or his realms.

"What do you want with me?" I asked, seeing now that he looked different, no longer dressed like a pirate. In fact, he looked more like the powerful Being I would have first expected, despite still not wearing the full form of his demon. Although, he had to be appreciated, for his muscular figure was most certainly one to be admired and lusted over, and had I been in the possession of a hand fan I would have used it for the purpose of cooling my sexual nature down.

But then this wasn't helped by being forced to look at his bare torso that was nothing short of incredible. Muscles upon muscles, most I didn't even have the brain power to recall the names of. I just knew which ones I liked best, and let's just say that he had them all and more!

He wore only one shoulder piece of armour, that was a series of hammered plates which were spiked on the top and curled around his large shoulder, one that looked just as powerful and strong had it been as bare as the other. Black straps of leather held it in place across his wide chest, they matched the thick belts that clung to a muscled stomach and his hips and held a long length of material in place. The dark red skirt was one that covered his legs and held a line of demonic symbols down the centre that was framed by glowing gold thread.

The hint of a flaming crown could be seen hovering over his head that was the shape of thorn entwined horns. He smirked at me before clearing his throat, as if amused he had caught me staring at his body the way I had. Then he sat down opposite me in a large throne like chair, making himself comfortable before starting to explain.

"Like I said, I have a proposition for you, Youngling."

"And that is?" I asked, not wanting to dance around the Maypole any longer than I needed to.

"I would like you to join my Royal Court," he said, making my mouth drop open.

"Uh… excuse me… did you say Royal Court and include the words like… me join you?" Again, he smirked, and I couldn't tell if it made him more dangerous looking or less so.

"I do not believe there is anything wrong with your hearing, Pipper," he replied in a knowing tone.

"I'm surprised you even know my name, let alone know that I'm an Imp, one that you're about to invite into your Royal Court."

"Your point being?" he asked, now curious.

"Well, excuse me for saying this, my Lord, but I find this hard to believe that you would want an Imp representing your court."

"And why not, for you are a Shadow Imp after all, and therefore you have as much right to be in my world just as any other, for you are practically classed as a demon yourself," he argued back his point, making me shrug my shoulders in return.

"That may be true but even to a demon I am classed as nothing more than a lowly creature, especially compared to the rest of those that sit in your court, and I may act of simple mind, my Lord, but I can assure you that I am not. So, why not tell me why is it you really want me to become part of your elite royal service," I said, cutting through the bullshit and making him grin because of it. Then he laughed and said,

"She said I would like you... for you are certainly a unique one, that is to be sure. Alright, little Imp, I will give you the answers you seek, if you first give me one of your own."

"And that is?" I asked.

"How did you do it?" I frowned in question, making him elaborate,

"I confess, I am surprised you have lasted this long."

"Abaddon." I said his name with longing as I looked towards the fancy golden arch that now decorated the doorway I knew led back into the tunnel.

"Now what I want to know is how you have survived when others have not?" he asked, making me release a sigh before being curious to ask,

"How do you think I did it?" At this, he took the time to contemplate my question, tapping at his lips for a few seconds before flicking his hand out in a gesture that told me he didn't know.

"Many think it is some kind of witchcraft or a casting made. Others believe it is through the grace of the Gods that you have been blessed or it is something else entirely."

"Something else?" I enquired.

"It is as my Chosen One stated in her dreams," he said, with his eyes burning brighter for a few seconds before simmering down back to their startling aqua tones.

"And that is what, my Lord?" At this, he shrugged his shoulder and said,

"You are fated to be his." I sucked in a surprised breath before it all started to make sense.

For this was why Lucifer was here now. He didn't want me on his Royal Court at all…

He wanted my Abaddon.

STEPHANIE HUDSON

NINETEEN

MY PAROLE

My Abaddon.

He wanted my fated Beast, and right now the only way to get him was... *through me.*

"You want to use me, use me to control the Beast?" I said, coming right out with it. He didn't deny it. No, instead he simply told me,

"I have been watching you for many years now, and the accounts that have reached my ears have both amazed and surprised me. And make no mistake, Imp, it is something that rarely happens, I can assure you."

"Oh, I believe it," I answered.

"However, I was also intrigued, for I did not believe that if his maker could not control him, that anything could… nothing until you, little Imp," he said, nodding my way and making the crown burn brighter, its flames licking at the air above him.

I released a frustrated sound and pushed my wild curly hair back, before telling him truthfully,

"You have this all wrong." At this, he raised a brow and enquired,

"How so?" So I told him,

"I don't control him." He frowned before shaking his head a little before telling me,

"I beg to differ, for was it not you that calmed him of his rage on many occasions before, the last of which caused about 80,000 human deaths in Shamakhi as a great earthquake ripped through the mortal realm… ah yes, I see now this concerns you."

"Gods," I whispered, as that knowledge rocked me to my core.

"I am sorry that happened, for I do not wish for lives to be lost or to weigh heavily on my own for his actions… that being said, I will remind you, my Lord, that I did not cause that, but you did by having me taken from him,"

I said, igniting his anger for a terrifying heartbeat as his eyes turned bloody and crimson. The crown also turned a deeper shade of red, and only calmed again once he took a deep breath as if trying to cool his own rage. Maybe he needed his own Chosen One to tame him?

"The outcome, I will admit, was surprising and not one I expected," he confessed with a slash of his hand.

"I know what you're doing," I said, once again being blunt.

"Really? Well, please enlighten me, little Imp."

"You think that you will be able to use him in your wars or your battles and I will be there to calm him down or to point him in the right direction for you. But I am here now to tell you that it won't happen." At this he seemed surprised, before that evil glint in his eyes started to glow again and let's just say, it was obvious he was not a Being who was used to being denied… *not by anyone.*

"I should warn you, Imp, saying no to your King quite often results in an untimely end and torturous death." At this I swallowed hard and decided again to play my last hand.

"That may be the end result for some, but with regard to myself, I am calling your bluff." On hearing this he raised an eyebrow at me, and thankfully this went back to amusing him.

"I don't think you'll kill me, because I think you know deep down what will happen if your creation wakes up and finds me gone for good... killed by your hand, no less... for he may seem too mindless with rage to comprehend your world, but that's where you would be wrong. And you know where that assumption will lead you?"

"Yes, and where is that?"

"Hell in ruins." At this, his face turned hard and he leaned forward in an intimidating way, before he said in a dangerous tone,

"Is that a threat, little Imp?"

"No, it's a promise and a fact, for he won't just tear this place apart looking for me, he will break free from it completely and where do you think he will go next? Where do you think he will take that rage, my Lord?" I asked, making him grit his teeth as my words sunk into a place I hoped they stayed.

"A rage that will tear through each realm like a never-ending storm until it has destroyed the entirety of Hell." He slashed an arm out in front of him and argued in vain,

"Nothing is that powerful."

"Are you so sure, and is that self-assured ego something you are willing to risk your entire kingdom on, my Lord, for I have seen but a glimpse of it." He scoffed at this and said,

"You know not of what you speak, Youngling."

"All respect, King, but I am the one who knows him unlike any other, so it would be a grave mistake to doubt of which I speak." At this, he got up in anger and shouted down at me,

"And this obliteration of my world, one you so wrongly assume to happen from one simple and meaningless death such as yours, tell me, you small being you… exactly what will happen to my world?" he said with a bite of anger, getting closer to me, for this last part was said only inches from my face, one I braved to meet head on. So, I gave it to him with a grit of my own teeth,

"He will grow bigger and stronger than you ever imagined possible… a demonic force fuelled by more fury than you could ever imagine! One that will never stop, not unless he has me. Now, answer me this, my Lord, just what do you think he would do to the one who took me from him… *to the one who killed me?*" I snarled this last sentence, making him growl.

"What will you do when you have nothing left to give him to cool his fury and put out the fires of that rage within him…?" I said, taking pause to get closer to him myself and becoming only a hairsbreadth away from his face, before threating him with a glimpse of his future,

"…*what will you do when you having nothing left to rule, Lucifer?*" I knew I had him at this, as he snarled at me with his demonic face taking hold for a few seconds before he tore himself away from me. Once distanced, I watched as his huge frame calmed enough to go back to his usual size, for in his rage his demon had started to come through, making him grow.

This was when I calmed my own tone enough to add,

"Are you really willing to forsake your entire world on a whim?" At this he looked back at me in a thoughtful manner, before he released a sigh and finally agreed,

"You're right, I cannot afford to kill you, for it is true what you say… I may need you in time, but you forget who it is you are speaking with, Imp, for I am not without my ways!" he snapped, making me flinch hoping this was him now just calling my bluff.

"There is no way, for I have nothing you can use against me… you have nothing to threaten or hold me to ransom with, for the only Being I care for is the very one you fear," I said, and his reaction surprised me as I had expected his anger not his sadistic, evil grin.

"And you are sure of that, are you?" he taunted.

"As sure as I know my own heart, for it beats for him." At this he smirked and said,

"And what if I told you of another fate the Gods had planned for you?" Now I had to confess this comment threw me into confusion.

"You are just trying to trick me, for there is no other fate for me but the one I have here with Abaddon."

"But that is where you are wrong again, young one, for it was the Oracle herself that set you on your path and it is one that does not end here, and it does not end with my Beast." At this I stood up quickly and shouted,

"You lie!" He chuckled, as he enjoyed my reaction, and shrugged his shoulder casually before telling me,

"And what pray do I have to gain from doing such, for I care little should you be fated to another, mortal, or demon alike... just so as long as you can control my own creation, I can assure you that I have no interest beyond that," he said in a calm tone that unfortunately told me he spoke the truth.

"I don't care what the Fates say, or the damn Oracle, for I…" I never got anything else out as I soon found myself pinned against the wall and lifted by a single hand that now collared my neck, choking me.

"Be very careful, Imp, for no one disrespects my queen, for I have tortured for far less than the bite of your words… remember that!" he snarled, before dropping me and leaving me trying to catch my breath again in a heap on the floor.

"Now, as for your uses, is this your final answer to which I demand of you?" I heaved in a sigh as I looked at the floor, watching as the angry tears fell and soaked into the carpet. Then I looked up at him from the floor and snapped,

"I will never help you control him… *Never!*" At this, he grinned down at me before lowering to rest his forearm on a bent knee, getting closer to my level.

"Now, who's to say I have not already discovered a way to calm the Beast, one that doesn't include you, a child of the elemental realm." I frowned before snarling,

"Nothing is strong enough." At this, he tapped my nose and made a tutting sound before telling me,

"There you go, breaking your own rules, Imp, by

letting assumption rule your mind's decisions… for it was true once, nothing was born strong enough… *not until this moment,*" he said, making me suck in a shocked breath. He rose up, pulling me up with him and the moment he let me go, I started staggering backwards. Because I knew now that I had to get back to Abaddon, for this suddenly felt like a trap.

"What, little Imp, did you think I wouldn't have a backup plan?" he taunted with a laugh. And I knew he was telling the truth because he was right. He wouldn't have come here without having something else planned. Because this was the King of Hell we were talking about, which meant I didn't really have a chance, and that in turn meant that I barely made it to the door before I was grabbed from behind. Then, after I was yanked back hard against his large body, one that towered over me, I let out a fearful breath.

"You said you would just leave," I stated, reminding him of his earlier promise.

"That I did, but alas, young one… I didn't say when I left that I wouldn't be taking you with me." I sucked back my shock, just as a figure emerged from nowhere. A being that was cloaked entirely in a dark blue cloth and was walking towards the tunnel. My mind started to panic at who or what that demon could do, and I just prayed to the Gods that whatever it was, it didn't hurt Abaddon. Something I once believed impossible. But then Lucifer had been right, assumption was a dangerous thought to have down in Hell. One that could get you killed along with those you cared for and right now in my life, there was only one.

"Abaddon." I whispered his name in a hopeless tone.

"Aww, come now, take comfort in knowing he will be none the wiser with you gone."

"Wwwhat doo you mean?" I asked, just as I saw the figure raising their hands up and after a blue light flashed from them, one bright enough to momentarily blind me, I blinked until my sight returned. And it found…

The impossible!

For there now, walking down the tunnel was none other than…

Me.

"No… it… it can't be," I stammered out, as a voice started to sing out his name… it was my voice… singing the name belonging to my Beast.

The last sight I saw before the door closed was that

the figure had fully transformed into a version of myself, down to my dress, hair, height, and weight… every single element of me was exactly the same.

"See, I told you I wasn't without my ways… for I always get what I want, Imp, *you will do well to remember that in the future,*" he said, lifting me up in his arms and whispering this last part of the threat in my ear.

"That won't hold him for long, he will know, he will know it isn't me," I said, as tears ran down my face and on to the arms that held me captured.

"Well, that just depends on you doesn't it, as I came to understand something after having you watched all of these years, Pipper…" I shook my head but didn't speak, allowing him to do so,

"…I realised it wasn't just the Beast that fell in love with the Imp… but more importantly for me, it was the Imp that fell in love with the Beast…" I shuddered in his hold as a sob tore through me, and once more he whispered the end of his sentence in my ear,

"*…that is where I knew my true power would lie.*" Then I felt him nod to where the imposter had left, making his painful point.

"No, please don't do this, don't take me away from

him... don't... I beg of you, I beg of you, my Lord, please let me stay with him!" I shouted, begging now, but he simply chuckled behind me in a cruel way before his lips were once more at my neck, as he kissed his way up to my ear.

"The way I see it, you have two choices, my girl, you can either control him for me or you will never see him again... it is your choice, for you are right, I will not kill you." I closed my eyes and shuddered out a cry, one that tore right through me like the Devil's own dagger was piercing my heart. Because I knew that I couldn't do it. I couldn't become what Lucifer wanted me to. Not to the one that I loved more than anything else in this world!

In all the worlds combined.

I couldn't become what I loathed Lucifer for doing to him.

I couldn't make him become the tool that Lucifer had created him for. I couldn't do that to him... because... *because I loved him.* Which meant that I would rather die and face an eternity without ever seeing him again, than make him into the monster everyone said he was.

Because he was so much more than that.

He was my Beast, and I was his Imp.

And our love was all that mattered.

"Very well, I see you have made your decision," he said after a sigh.

"What happens now?" I asked through my tears.

"Well, I am hoping that I will not need you to control him, for I trust my shape shifter will do just as fine a job as you."

"It won't work," I said again, making him tell me,

"Well, only time will tell now, wont it? Either way, your fate has been decided once more, little one."

I swallowed hard and asked,

"And that is?"

"Like I said, I am not foolish enough to kill you, as you will be my backup plan if things go wrong. But I can't have you running around in Hell either, so consider this your parole, Imp…"

"My parole?" This turned out to be my last question before my world once more was ripped from me and completely changed, this time filling me full of a new heartache as the Devil told me…

"You're getting out, little Imp, and for once, it's on…

Good behaviour."

TWENTY

TALL HELLISH TALES
PRESENT DAY

"**O**h no! That's… That's…" After I had finished telling this part of my story, a little sob hiccupped from Amelia and made me feel so guilty that I scooped her up into my arms and cuddled her to me.

"Hey, come on now… what are your mum and dad gonna think if they know that I've upset you?" I asked softly, as I rocked my body putting weight from one to foot to the other.

"But the Devil, he made you leave your Beast, just… just like Gaston did." I smiled at her words seeing how full of compassion and love she was, even at such a young age and it made me feel all warm and gooey inside.

She was beautiful through and through.

"Yes, that's true and what he did was wrong. But the most important lesson here is that he learned from his mistakes," I told her, knowing that in life, this was perhaps one of the most important lessons anyone could learn.

"And he was bad, like being grounded, type of bad," she said in an angry tone, one which said that had the Devil been here in front of her now she would have said the same thing to him, reprimanding him in the cutest way possible. I had to say, the idea of anyone grounding the Devil and sending him to his room to sulk… oh yeah, I would have paid good money for that one!

"Again, this is true, but we have to remember the second part of the story, *which is the happiest part,*" I said, whispering this last part to her as I put her down, and doing so with a wink at the end.

"What's that?" she asked, now rubbing away her tears with her arm after making a snuffling sound as kids often did when upset.

"Well, it's when I met Adam, silly Billy dinky pants." She giggled after this, and I was just happy that she had a smile back on her face again. Oh, and just in time to, as we were about to walk into the dining room where she would be having lunch. Of course, the moment I opened the doors and walked into the large lavish dining room, my eyes only went to one place. It was a room that was used on a daily basis these days, due to how many people that now lived in Afterlife. Because once the King had announced that Afterlife would become their family home, it became a hub for everyone else to flock to. This was because the King of Kings had not declared one place his home for centuries, not since he had once been the King of Persia.

But since meeting his Chosen One, things had changed dramatically for the King, starting with staying in one place indefinitely. Of course, he would still have to leave on occasion to conduct business and what not, but he loathed to be without his family. This meant his trips were usually swift and concluded within twenty-four hours, or when that wasn't practical it became a family affair. These were also usually the times that my snuggle bunny would surprise me with a trip or something else that would mean just the two of us.

Basically, in the nuttiest of shells, life wasn't just good, it was the best! It was more than I could have ever hoped for and now, looking at that chair and seeing it empty for the first time, I felt like I was fucking it up all over again!

Now, getting back to the dining room, and let's just say that mealtimes had become quite an event. Because there was the King's council and those that lived here who had soon become family after Keira and Dom had united as not only man and wife but also as King and Queen.

Of course, Toots never really went in for all that royal lark, as she called it. In her words, she just married the man she loved and everything else that came with that was secondary. This meant that Toots still got all embarrassed when anyone would curtsy or call her queen and all the other royal stuffiness. However, it was clear that her husband enjoyed watching his wife squirm because of this, and the smirk he always tried to hide behind his hand was fooling no one.

In fact, he was similar to my Adam in that way, as it wasn't often you found the King distracted enough not to notice everything his wife did, as it was clear he was hopelessly besotted. And why not, for she was totally awesome and my bestie for a reason, her and Sophia, as she was also cool as shit... although, thinking on it, that wasn't a flattering saying to call my other bestie. Maybe leaving the shit out of it as, after all, Sophia was a huge germaphobe, which me and Toots used to find hilarious seeing as she's one of the most powerful demons and all… oh and most likely the cleanest, I thought with a sneaky giggle.

Speaking of which, Sophia looked up from her place at the table and after glancing at the empty seat Adam usually sat at, she looked back at me. Then she silently told me,

'It will be okay'. I nodded my head a little in thanks, and after Toots witnessed this little exchange she was out of her chair like a shot and rushing over to me.

"Don't worry, men always get hungry, he will be back soon," she said as soon as she made it over to me, pulling me in for a hug. After this we were joined by another presence, one that became known to us when Amelia shouted with joy,

"Daddy!" Mr tall, dark, and royal handsome man quickly swooped his daughter up into his arms like he always did. It was at this point that the King, one I was definitely now more used to, came over and like I often did with his child, he ruffled her hair and said,

"Hello, my beautiful young lady, I would ask what you have been doing with your day but seeing as you have paint behind your ears, *I think I know.*" He whispered this last part by her neck before blowing raspberries there and making her howl with laughter... she was almost as ticklish as I was.

"Daddy, stop... no... he he!" she complained in between her giggles. I looked to Keira who clearly adored the sight of her husband with their daughter, as her eyes always got soft like that when watching the two of them. This, of course, meant that she didn't mind at all that Amelia was clearly a daddy's girl.

I asked her once why she didn't get jealous and she said,

"Because I know my time will come when she is older and wants to do girly stuff... although, I might miss seeing ribbons in Draven's hair or makeup on his face sat at one of her famous tea parties, as I can't see her still doing this when she is a teenager, can you?" Of course my answer had been to burst out laughing, as the one time I too had seen this had brought tears to my eyes, it had been that funny.

But then again, there wasn't much that Dom wouldn't do for his little girl. Basically, he was just a big push over, and often it was Keira who had to bring out the parenting big guns.

As for now, it was Dom whose hand I felt clasped at my shoulder before he told me,

"Have no fear, Pipper, I have spoken with Adam and be assured he just needs time, for I am afraid your latest antic really… well, for lack of a better term, ruffled some feathers."

"But he doesn't have feathers because he doesn't have wings, silly," Amelia said, looking up at her daddy who was still holding her to one side of him with an arm around her. The look of love he gave her was one that was a usual sight to see.

"That's true, how could I forget these things, but then again, I'm lucky because I have you to help me remember," he teased, tapping his own head and making her giggle. But then, after this, her mood changed as if she'd remembered something and suddenly she frowned at him, now looking very cross indeed. This was naturally an 'uh oh' moment for me.

Dom looked taken aback and said,

"Now that is a curious look, little one… come on, out with it… what have I done this time, for those type of looks are only usually reserved *for your mother*." He whispered this last part, and I could see her lips twitching as she tried to stay angry.

"You have a lot of explaining to do, Mister," she stated in a firm sweet voice, making me laugh and Toots reprimand her,

"Now watch your tone, Missy." Meanwhile, Dom looked as if he was barely containing his laughter trying to take her annoyance with him seriously.

"And prey tell me, pretty child of mine, exactly what explaining do I have to do this time, for I have a feeling someone has been telling tall Hellish tales again." At this point, I lifted up my hands when he shot me a questioning look, knowing exactly who the culprit was for these tall Hellish tales.

"Hey, don't shoot the messenger, I was merely telling your daughter a totally innocent fairy tale... *of sorts.*" I muttered this last part to myself. But then came the next question to ask, and I tensed knowing what it would be before my very powerful King said,

"Um, and what fairy tale was this I wonder?" This was when I fessed up with a well-known Pip catch phrase...

"Erh... My Bad."

TWENTY ONE

ANOTHER HANDSOME KING

Toots shook her head at me, as she usually did when trying to tell me that saying 'my bad' wouldn't get me out of everything. So, I released a sigh and said,

"The story is only my version of Beauty and the Beast, with maybe a little King Kong thrown in there, because seriously, who do you think gave them the idea?" At this Amelia giggled.

"And this story of yours, I gather it has not painted me in the best light." The King pressed on, and I released a sigh before Amelia was the one to intervene on my behalf, and doing so in the funniest way possible.

"We all make mistakes, Daddy," Amelia said, this time making Keira burst out laughing, ending in a very Toots' like snort. But then Dom shot her a look too, making her cough back her laughter and try hopelessly to hide her amusement by looking serious…

Man, parenting was tough.

"Don't worry about it, Dom, I painted the Devil in a far worse light than you," I said, making him close his eyes and pinch the bridge of his nose in frustration, like he always did. As for his daughter, Amelia pulled his hand down, got close to his face and said,

"It's okay, Daddy, Pip said the Devil was Gaston, not you, so you're safe from my wrath." At this, he raised an eyebrow at her before shaking his head as if asking himself what was he to do with his little girl. Then he looked to his wife, and she held up her hands telling him,

"Hey, don't look at me, I'm the youngest one here that she spends any time with, and how often do you think it is I say the word wrath, huh?"

"She's got a good point… she never says it," I said, sticking up for Toots. Dom's lips twitched with his amusement that eventually gave way to a full grin. That was until Amelia continued down the road of reprimanding her father and said,

"It will be okay, Daddy, just promise that you will never send Pip to Hell again and say you're sorry, and all will be forgiven." At this he emitted a little growl, one that his wife and his daughter knew never to take seriously.

"Now, that's not nice and Mummy always says to say sorry when you have been bad or naughty."

"I will remember that one, mark my words, wife of mine," Dom said, after getting close to Keira so he could whisper this mischievous threat in her ear, making her blush. Then he kissed her heated cheek and turned his attention back to his daughter when she said,

"Come on, Daddy, I know you can do it." I had to clear my throat at this one to stop all the laughter I could feel bubbling up and ready to burst out. I mean, who knew that hundreds of years later and the King of Kings would be manipulated by a three-year-old into saying sorry to me. In fact, had my snookie bear not been angry with me, then this would have been a contender for the most awesome day of the week award.

"Alright, I will make you a deal, if you eat all of your broccoli and at least five pieces of carrot, then I will apologise," Dom said, like a true parent bribing their children.

"A quarter of my broccoli and three carrots," was Amelia's counter deal, doing as I taught her, which was to always bargain for what you want.

"Half the broccoli and four carrots," Dom said, trying to hold back on laughing as he continued to conduct this veggie related business deal. At this, Amelia smirked and nodded. Dom then put her down and she held out her hand to her father and said,

"Deal, now let's shake on it and be done." Again, the King's lips twitched as he looked down at his daughter, knowing full well the reason she spoke like this, as Keira was right… but then again, *she usually was.*

"Deal, now hop to it, little one," Dom said, giving her bum a little tap to get her moving towards the table, where a plate of food was covered with a silver dome, waiting for her. But then she turned around and cocked a hand on her hip, now tapping her little foot impatiently,

"I think you're forgetting your part of the deal, Daddy." At this, Dom released a sigh before turning to me and saying,

"Mrs Winifred Pipper Ambrogetti, I sincerely apologise

for sending you to Hell, where you met your fated Beast and the events that followed which led you to your Chosen One, Adam."

"That's not how it's supposed to go!" Amelia complained, folding her little arms.

"Ah, but you're forgetting, sweetheart, that is exactly how it went," Dom said with a wink, and at this Little Bean screwed her face up as if she was thinking really hard about something before she then said,

"Half of my broccoli and two carrots." Then she walked off towards the table, leaving Dom chuckling and Toots now being the one to shake her head as if she didn't know what to do with her daughter.

"She gets it from you," Keira said to her husband when he approached, wrapping an arm around her and pulling her tight against him,

"Beauty from her mother, and formidable in business just like her father, I believe the Gods have blessed us indeed," he said, making her grin up at him.

"That was smooth, Kingio, real smooth," I said, nudging his arm making Keira laugh. After this the three of us made our way to the table where Sophia and her husband, Zagan, were already there talking with Amelia and asking her about her day. Vincent, her uncle, and also the King's brother, was also in attendance and someone who I could see was sneaking vegetables from her plate. Then he would wink down at her and place a finger to his lips like it was a secret, making her giggle behind her hand.

As for me, well I spent the entire time unable to eat a thing and looking longingly at the door in hopes that Adam would come back.

Unfortunately, this didn't happen.

And just like I had felt that first day back in the mortal realm…

It was as though I had lost my greatest love all over again.

DERBYSHIRE
9TH OCTOBER 1680

The day I came back was the very same day I proved my point.

Lucifer had made a mistake.

Now, upon first opening my eyes, I didn't know many of the details surrounding it, for example I didn't know how long it was before Abaddon realised the impostor wasn't me, but I had a pretty good idea that it was a lot quicker than Lucifer ever imagined it would be.

This was confirmed very quickly after finding myself waking up in yet another room I had never seen before. I had to say, that waking up and not knowing where I was would have been classed as a habit, had not nearly eighty years gone by since the last time this happened. Because this time, well all I could say was that where I was now was somewhere very grand, somewhere very expensive and somewhere that no doubt belonged to a king of some sort.

The theme of the room was definitely one of my favourite colour pallets, being that it matched my eyes. A feature that I happened to like on myself. It was a vivid forest green with blue accents around the room, and what I liked to call colours of the peacock.

It also seemed as if fashion had changed somewhat since the last time I was amongst humans. As now these great drapes that hung down and framed the large windows, were fabrics to be seen elsewhere in the room, now matching other elements, like the coverings on the bed and cushions on the seats. There were even swags of the same material that hid the doors behind them, no doubt done in an attempt was ward off the draught from the winter months.

"This would make beautiful coloured hair," I said as my first thing in the mortal realm in what must have been nearly eighty years. It also made me wonder if one day someone would invent a way to dye hair the same lush and vibrant colours that surrounded me today, just as they could with fabrics. That would certainly be a day to remember for me.

I swung the covers back and got out of the large bed, stretching and yawning as I did so. And it had to be said that despite missing the luxury of an actual bed it was not enough for regret…

Not nearly enough.

For I would never regret my time spent in Hell, for no amount of luxury could make up for what I had now lost, for the pain of which was only now just sinking in.

"Abaddon." I uttered his name just as I sank to the floor to my knees, where I bowed my head, now cradling it in my own hands as I wept. I remembered little after Lucifer had granted me my release, as once again being under his control I must have been rendered unconscious for him to get me back to the mortal realm. I suppose we

all had our secrets, and Lucifer was no different. For it was clear he would not have wanted me to see how he had created a portal so easily... a rare and extremely powerful gift indeed, and a secret kept for good reason.

But now I was back.

And my first act in the mortal realm was a pitiful one. Because I don't know how long I sat there and cried for, but it was almost as if someone was giving me the chance to mourn my loss. I knew this, for the moment I had finished, and my tears had all but dried up and left me, was when I finally heard something other than my own misery.

And I knew that when someone did finally discover me here, all they would find was nothing left but an empty husk. A feeling as though I was a shell of myself with no hope in sight. In fact, I was starting to wonder if I shouldn't just go out there and commit some random act of horror against the human race just so I could find myself back in Hell once more.

A single thought that almost turned itself into an absolute when suddenly I heard the unlocking of a door. This was before that same length of material was pushed back and in walked a Being I had not seen for a long time. And well, considering we were in the mortal realm, this made it all the more shocking, making me shout out his name the second I saw the very last King I ever expected to see...

"Asmodeus!"

TWENTY TWO

LUCIFER'S MISTAKES

"Asmodeus!"

I shouted his name in shock, wondering what it must have taken to get him here, for I knew that the Devil's kings and the rulers of these realms of Hell rarely left… and for good reason. They were stronger in their own territories but also, no one wanted to leave their own kingdom without its ruler for long, and although time worked differently in the mortal realm than it did in Hell, there were many variations to this, because it all depended on where you were, for some places in Hell could mean that a month could equate to a single day passing for humans. Naturally, this also worked the other way around for years in the mortal realm could be but one in Hell. It was the same with the Elemental Realms, along with the Shadowlands, which in themselves were classed as being in Hell as much as they weren't… simply put, it was all so confusing.

But despite all of this, here Asmodeus stood, and now very much looking the part of 17th century nobility. He wore a long open jacket that was purple with a silver brocade design. Underneath this, he wore a long waistcoat that was a darker shade than his jacket, and had a line of round silver buttons embossed with what I assumed was the Draven family crest. Dark breaches and shoes completed the outfit, that were of a type I gathered were typical of the fashion these days. Again, his dark curls were pulled back from his face, showing off the handsome lines of his strong jaw. High cheekbones combined with a fine figure stood up proud and straight, which was a position that spoke of power, confidence, and an attractive arrogance that his situation as a royal granted him.

In short, the King looked good… *better than good.*

"What are you doing here?" I asked, getting back to the important question and blushing, considering the last time

I saw him he had kissed me.

"Did I not say until next time, pretty girl, for here you are, alive and well… if not a little sombre," he said, adding this last part as if he could still see what remained of my tears.

"I am not exactly well, far from it after Lucifer cast me out," I said bitterly.

"Ah yes, the Beast… and of course the very reason I am here now," he said, piquing my interest instantly and making me shout,

"Abaddon!" He paid no attention to this, so I quickly continued,

"That's why you're here? Is he alright? What happened? Did he discover that it wasn't me, that I am not there, that there was an impostor?! By the Gods, please tell me!" All these questions came out of me in a rush, and Asmodeus held up his hands as if in surrender and started laughing.

"Easy, young one, take a breath before you find yourself unconscious once more, and not from my kiss this time." I blushed again at the reminder before doing as I was told and deflating back onto the bed. But this must have been like a red flag to a bull for the King of Lust, as his eyes started to glow just as Lucifer's had when he was angry.

However, he clearly had great restraint, for he didn't make an inappropriate move.

Then after releasing a sigh, he said,

"I see you took my advice quite literally. I have to say, I was greatly impressed."

"Impressed?" I questioned.

"Well, there are not many who can contain such a beast as Abaddon with merely their wits and their charms to aid them… so yes, naturally I was greatly impressed, for you must be one *hell of a dancer,* and I mean that in the most literal sense, of course." At this, I laughed as it was surprising because Dominic Draven's father was actually quite funny and had a great sense of humour. He also looked incredibly handsome too when he had mirth dancing in his eyes.

"I fell in love with him," I admitted with a sigh, and this was when Asmodeus came further into the room and occupied a seat closest to the bed.

"As it was fated to be, and just as this is now, young one." I frowned at this.

"You think it was fated for Lucifer to cast me out of Hell?" The shock in my tone would have been hard to miss.

"But of course."

"But why!? It makes no sense. First everyone is telling me it is fated for me to get sentenced to Hell for a crime I didn't fully commit by myself. And that includes your own daughter, no less," I said, making him nod as if he already knew this, before I carried on with my rant,

"So, Sophia tells me to basically take my punishment without a fight, so I did. Then you and your dear friend, Lucifer, decide to punish me by sending me to the deepest levels of Hell, but this is a fine outcome right, for it was all fated…" I say, getting lost in my tale of woe.

"It was fated," he stated, making me huff,

"Fated that I might become food for an uncontrollable beast that Lucifer had created? Fated for me to dance for him, to entertain him and make him fall in love with me before I then fell in love with him back!"

"Again, my answer remains the same, child," he said, making me go on to prove my point.

"Then if that is so, and my fate was always to calm the beast so that everyone in Hell may find peace for 80 years, then answer me… why was it then fated for me to be cast out of hell and leave him again…? Why, with the grace of the Gods that reside in both Heaven and Hell, why would that have all been fated, if by the end I was forced to leave?!" I said, shouting all of this speech and now feeling exhausted by it. However, Asmodeus' reaction surprised me.

"I often chuckle whenever I hear the mortal term 'God acts in mysterious ways', for is not the Gods but it is the Fates. You could spend a mortal eternity questioning their motives, questioning their reasonings for such things and contemplating what their outcomes will be to such decisions made… but that, my pretty girl, would no doubt turn you more insane than any eternity faced in Hell." I let my once tense shoulders slump in defeat and agreed,

"You're right about that." Then, after a moment of silence passed between us, I looked to the window, seeing the sun was close to setting over what looked like English countryside.

"Where are we, anyway?" I asked.

"The place my son currently resides in, after first convincing its mortal owners that the building was crumbling and not fit to live in… alas, as you can see, it is not that way at all. However, it served a purpose during this time for him to be in Derbyshire, and I hear that Chatsworth House has been home to royalty before and therefore was fitting for such a King, don't you think?"

Of course, I knew what he referred to, as this grand house was a castle in its own right, and had once been where Elizabeth I had ordered for Mary, Queen of Scots to be imprisoned. This was after she abdicated and fled from Scotland to England in 1567.

"Alright, so now that question has been answered, now it is time for my next and the most obvious of all, why are you here, Asmodeus?"

"As I stated, I am simply here to grant you a message."

"And that is?" I asked, hoping he would hurry up already and do so.

"Let's just say there is a reason there was a massive earthquake today in Malaga, Spain, which ended up destroying a great proportion of the city."

"Abaddon... *he knows,*" I whispered as my heart ached for him. Asmodeus bowed his head in acknowledgement, and I couldn't help it as a tear slipped through beneath my lashes. I guess they hadn't dried up after all, I thought bitterly.

"So, does this mean that Lucifer wants me back?" I asked in a hopeful tone.

"Not exactly." His answer surprised me, for surely the plan was not to let Abaddon continue on his furious rampage.

"What then, what exactly does he expect me to do? I can't calm him down if I'm not there!" I snapped.

"Lucifer has, should we say… had a change of heart." Again, my face was easy to read as my frown deepened.

"I don't understand, I mean for one, I didn't actually think he had a heart." At this, Asmodeus chuckled.

"As hard as it may be to believe, he does indeed have a heart. However, there is only one being alive that it belongs to and seeing as it's not a love that is yet in a position to be returned…well, let's just say it can make the ruler of Hell somewhat bitter… something I am not in a habit of hastily admitting, having some experience with this myself," he said, rubbing the back of his neck in a frustrated manner, and I had to say I was surprised.

I was surprised for a number of reasons. In fact, at the top of that list would be discovering that Lucifer could actually be in love with someone. Second, that this shock would be to discover that Asmodeus had also lost his heart to someone and was admitting so, not only to his friend but to himself also. Because if there was one thing I knew about royalty of any kind, it was that they admitted no weaknesses, for to do so was like handing defeat to the enemies on a platter.

Then again, I was just a lowly Imp, and not strong enough to be considered anyone's enemy, so was it really so surprising? Hell, if I had to name even one person I was an enemy to, I would be naming myself. Yet, despite knowing this and spending my near entire existence being my own worst enemy, as for right now, well I knew that none of this was my fault. No, for this situation had been by the bad decisions made by others, and now they were asking me to what, to help them!? To help them contain the consequence of their grave mistakes made. Had I not wanted to be reunited with Abaddon so badly then I would have told them to go back to Hell... *literally.*

"I warned Lucifer what would happen should he split us apart. I warned him and he didn't listen," I told Asmodeus with a shake of my head.

"I know this. as, trust in me when I tell you, the results of such were greatly discussed... in detail."

"And this great discussion, where exactly did it lead, huh? Was it somewhere along the lines of, 'oh darn, that Imp was right, and I was wrong, and I wish I would have listened to her, she is so unbelievably smart... a lot smarter than I'... something like that perhaps?" I questioned, making Asmodeus laugh.

"Not exactly, no," he replied with a smirk.

"Didn't think so," I said in cutting tone.

"Although, something has to be said for your nature and credit needed to be given by Lucifer when due, for there are not many that would go up against Lucifer and speak to him the way that you did. In his own words, he believed you to be both one of the most foolish and yet the most courageous demons he had ever met. And believe me when I tell you that is high praise indeed when coming from my friend." I scoffed at this, even if the truth was that it did make me feel good.

"So, what next? Where does that leave us and what is Lucifer's great plan this time?" I asked, rolling my wrist and making a sarcastic gesture with my hand.

"Lucifer has decided that it would be safer for everyone to get Abaddon out of Hell," Asmodeus said, shocking me beyond belief!

"What!" I screeched before taking another second to be sure I heard correctly.

"Is he crazy?" I asked, making Asmodeus hold up a hand as if silently asking for my patience so he could explain.

"He feels as though it is time for his creation to be joined with his host, a mortal vessel." At this, my mouth literally dropped open and for a few moments I must have looked like a dying fish thrown on the banks of the river Thames, for my mouth would open and close only to then repeat this motion over, for there were no words yet. Then finally after a time I hissed,

"*Is something like that even possible?*"

"The Fates seemed to think so," he answered with a shrug of his shoulders. This was when things started to click into place as I remembered my conversation not long ago with Lucifer.

"This was his backup plan wasn't it, or should I say the backup plan for his backup plan?" Asmodeus granted me a knowing look, giving me my answer before he spoke.

"It is true, when Lucifer learned that fate may have a mortal in mind, one that was said to be strong enough to hold him and contain his creation, he became intrigued by the idea. However, not being one to put all his faith in the Fates, he decided to first test this theory and whilst doing so, trying his luck at controlling you or should I say, controlling the Beast through you."

"And he did so knowing that if neither one worked, the outcome that was fated would happen anyway," I said, finishing off for him.

"Precisely," he agreed.

"So now what... what part in this exactly does he expect me to play now?"

"Is it not obvious?" he said smirking.

"Not to me."

"Being fated to Abaddon means that you are the only being capable of finding his vessel, and hopefully doing so before he destroys the entirety of Hell, for I believe we are under some urgency, as I'm sure you can imagine." Asmodeus said, with a slight cock of his head and stretching his neck to the side. If I knew him well enough, I may have said the gesture looked as if he was under slight stress. No doubt he was eager to get back to his own realm.

"Yeah, I can imagine easily enough having witnessed the result of finding me gone before," I commented, making him bow his head at me for he had obviously heard of the first time I was taken.

"So exactly how long do I have to search the entire mortal world looking for one human?" I asked sarcastically.

"A little over a month." His reply had me sitting straight up and tense in a heartbeat.

"What!" I shouted before shaking my head. "No... no, no, you have to be speaking in jest, for it cannot be done!?"

He shrugged his shoulders and told me,

"I only wish I was, but alas no, for Lucifer currently has him in a part of Hell that will take him a day to destroy before he then moves on, and when he does, he will break through the barriers Lucifer has had cast, and he will tear his way through the entire Kingdom, including that of your own, for where do you think he will go next but to the Elemental Realms in search of you." I knew this was true as I had told Abaddon everything there was to know about my life. After all, nearly eighty years with someone was a long time... and I talked... *a lot.*

"So, what you're basically saying is that the fate of our world now lies on my shoulders, and I have to find this mystery man, one that I will want to spend the rest of my life with... doing all this in just a month... do I have that right?"

"Yes, pretty girl, that is precisely what I am saying."

"Oh well, if that's all then," I replied sarcastically, throwing my hands up in a dramatic fashion before falling back onto the bed and covering my face, wondering if this nightmare would ever end.

"I don't exactly know the numbers, considering I've only just got back to the mortal realm, but the last time I was here there was over half a billion humans living in this realm. Now, assuming that Abaddon doesn't want to live in a female vessel for the rest of his life, and I don't want to bat for the other side, we can halve that number."

"Imp..." I held up my hand and said,

"Then, let us take out all the elderly and all the young... I think you can see where I'm going with this in proving my point that there is still an incredibly large number, and one that is well into the millions, Asmodeus."

"You will have help," he stated.

"Great and when you say help, do you mean like a lighthouse built by the Gods that will shine a light on this unfortunate soul?" I asked, making him grant me a look.

"An attitude shrouded in defeat will not help you, my dear."

"Oh, I'm sorry, yes, because it's going to be a positive mental attitude that's going to help me find this cock in a world sized haystack!" I shouted, now losing my temper. To give him his due, he didn't get angry in return and that only made me feel guilty.

"Forgive me, I don't mean to be rude, but I have had quite possibly the worst day ever, and nothing short of the Gods shining down a beam of light from Heaven onto this guy, is going to make it possible to find him. Surely you see that, as I ask you, how in the Gods am I going to find this person when I don't even know where to start?" I said, making him grant me soft look of understanding before telling me the only positive in this.

"I didn't say you had nowhere to start from, little one, for the Oracle has given some indication of where you will need to be."

"Oh, that's good of her," I muttered mockingly.

"And like I said, you will have help for I've instructed my son to grant you someone he trusts... *unequivocally.*"

"Who?" I asked, wondering now if they expected me to go running around the place not looking for only one person but now a second.

"You will find out soon enough, but I have been assured by many accounts that if there is one being capable enough to get certain jobs done, then he is the demon of choice." I wasn't sure I liked the sound of this, but then again, what little choice did I have?

"And this list of talents of his, I don't suppose being able to sniff out future husbands is one of them?" At this, he laughed and said after standing up,

"I like that, in fact I am going to take great pleasure in relaying this conversation to Lucifer myself, especially that last part. Now, if you'll excuse me, I will take my leave of you." I was about to get up myself when he held out his palm to me, gesturing for me to stay where I was. Then he told me,

"If I may suggest something, it will be for you to get some more sleep, for the next time you wake, that lighthouse you spoke so highly of will have already cast its beam on you and will take you to the very city where you will find him."

"It will?" At this, he nodded as he walked from the room, but then stopped long enough to say,

"Remember, pretty girl, trust your instincts and let them guide you, for they will aid you greatly when making your choice. It is not someone you will be attracted to, but more someone you will be consumed by, just as you were consumed by the Beast and gave your heart freely, you will want to do so with this man…"

"And how do you know that?" I asked in a small vulnerable voice, one he smiled at before telling me,

"Because the Fates have deemed it so and as you know, little one…

"The Fates do not lie."

TWENTY THREE

FATED HEARTACHE
COVENT GARDEN
9TH OCTOBER 1680

I had to confess I was surprised not only to be back in London, but also to find myself in a place I had rarely visited whilst living here. The reason for this was that there had been little cause for me to come to this area of London, being that it was known for its expensive homes. But despite that, even I could see that during the prison time I had served, it had changed. So much in fact, that at first I had questioned which part of London I was standing in as I hardly recognised it. For what once held wealthy homes, now held a small open market that from the smell of things, sold mainly fruit and vegetables. What surrounded this was now taverns, theatres, coffee houses and what looked to be brothels. Which is why I now very much doubted that the wealthy still lived here.

As for the market, it was most likely alive and teeming with activity in the light of day. But as for now, after the sun had given way to the night, it was currently a vast open space that was void of life. As for me, I had been dumped off to one side in a dark part of the alley that faced this space. Of course, I questioned why here? Why I had closed my eyes like Asmodeus had suggested I do and woke to find myself in a place I seemingly had no connection with?

Unsurprisingly, I had no one around to answer these questions, so I was left only to assume. Covent Garden was a district in London on the east fringes of the West End between Saint Martins lane and Drury Lane and again, an area I had spent little time in, which, I had to admit, made me feel even more out of my depth. In fact, I was feeling more alone now than ever before, and that was including the first day of my sentence in Hell.

Yet Asmodeus had assured me that fate would bring me here for a reason, and I could only hope that the reason was to find the vessel of the man I was supposed to fall in love with. One strong enough to be able to join him with the beast I had already fallen in love with.

I swear, even Shakespeare couldn't have written it and he was good. Of course, he'd be long gone by now, the thought was a sad one for I did indeed enjoy his plays. As for right now, and leaving Shakespeare out of it, I was down an alleyway adjacent to one of the taverns, a place I didn't yet know the name of. However, what I did know was that it was late in the evening, late enough for a group of men to stagger from its doors after clearly having one too many drinks.

And unfortunately for me, *I did not go unnoticed.*

"Look what we've got 'ere lads," one of the biggest of the four said, nudging the one closest to him.

"Great, I am back for five minutes and the first mortals I am faced with is you yaldsons!" I commented drily, calling them sons of prostitutes, which I was hoping was still an insult people used in today's society. I soon got my answer as their faces twisted in anger.

"Oh, you're gonna pay for that one!"

"Yeah, with her cunt!" another said, as all four came closer.

"No, Jimmy, you stay and keep watch," the big bastard said, motioning towards the end of the alleyway to the skinniest member with a nod.

"And what 'bout my cock, it needs shining just as much as the next man," he complained, when the big one grabbed his jacket and snarled down at him,

"You will have your turn fillin' her holes just after I have had a turn and they ain't as tight." He then sniggered before the one called Jimmy nodded and was on his way to keep watch, which was when I knew I needed to ditch these fuckers... and without a weapon, it was unlikely I was able to do so as easily as I would have liked.

So, I released a deep sigh and rolled my neck, knowing I didn't exactly have time for a brawl, but then again, it seemed I didn't have much time for anything these days.

So, I cracked my knuckles and motioned them forward.

"Come on then, dickwads, let's play." Hearing this new name and not understanding it, as clearly it was one of mine that hadn't taken off during my absence, I muttered...

"*All that work lost...* it means you're assholes, okay," I explained, making them come at me.

"I will warn you, fellas, I am a wee bit rusty, so bear with me... Whoa!" I said when the big one punched me in the stomach, and I doubled over coughing. Then, when he grabbed my hair and yanked me back up, I started laughing before telling him,

"Oh wait, I remember now." Then I uppercut him, catching his nose and feeling the bone move under my knuckles, and not in the way that it ever should naturally.

"Aww, look, I made you more handsome," I mocked as he dropped to the floor, now holding his broken face, and moaning in pain. I snorted a laugh and stepped over him ready for the next fucker on my shit list. Then as the next guy, let's call him Toothy as most were missing, came at me and I ducked out of the way of the next swing, spinning and kicking the guy in the back so he went down. This was after stumbling over where his friend had dropped holding his nose.

"Two down, now what you got for me shorty?" I asked the smaller one, who decided to run at me like a bull charging. So, this was when I ran at the wall using it to gain height before I hammered my fist down sideway across his face, using more force to break his jaw. He stumbled to the side, and I didn't dally around to wait for any of them to get back up, so I ran to the end of the alley and when I saw the scrawniest one out of the bunch of dickless grapes, I tapped him on the shoulder.

"Yoo-hoo." Then when he turned to look at me, I punched him in the face, making the pipe he was smoking throw up sparks in his face. After this, I heard a rush of angry shouts coming from the men in the alleyway and just as the guy slid down the wall he had been leaning against, I grabbed his wide brimmed hat and lifted it up in a gesture of thanks.

"That's my curtain call, bean pole!" I named him, before popping the hat on my head and picking up my skirts to run for it. And wasn't it just grand, for my first day back, and I had already been attacked and now being chased through the streets.

"Jeez, talk about a welcome home, Winnie," I muttered, as I ran towards Drury Lane only to find a new building I hadn't seen before. It was a large theatre set well back from the broader streets, and was accessed by narrow passages between the surrounding buildings.

"THERE SHE IS!" I heard shouted behind me, making me glance back to find them still chasing me. Well, it was clear men hadn't discovered a drink to make them smarter yet, for stupidly, one beating obviously wasn't enough for them. Which meant only one thing…

I needed a weapon.

So, I decided that in the theatre was probably my best chance at hiding until I could find something to defend myself with. Especially when seeing that now my pursuers had obviously decided to hang back due to the large amount of people that were now coming out of the theatre's front doors. A recent play had obviously just finished, and I thought the timing couldn't have been better. This was when I noticed a side door, one I knew was probably used for the theatre staff, including its performers.

The door was locked but thankfully all it needed was a good kick for it break open. Of course, this didn't exactly tickle as pain vibrated up my leg. But then I wasn't surprised, seeing as I had long been without shoes as these had been the first thing stolen when I had been forced to work in the prison's pits. But quite honestly, I was surprised my dress could still be classed as much. Especially considering I'd had this single garment for decades. In fact, the skirt had been getting shorter and shorter as the years passed, for it had been the first place to fray and tear.

Still, at the very least it was still somewhat clean, for I did try and take care of it while in Hell. But enough of the history of my dress, because it and me both stepped inside and found a maze of rooms and hallways. In fact, it was when turning down one of these particular hallways that I had to stop for fear of being seen as I could hear an exchange between two people, one that started with a knock on a door.

"Miss Margaret, it is I, Fitzwilliam." As soon as I heard this voice something in me was startled. I actually jerked back until my back hit the wall.

"Gods," I whispered in my shock, now holding a hand to my heart as if something had just touched it, making it beat faster than ever before. It had such an effect on me that I even found myself questioning my own sanity. It was almost like I was hearing a man's voice for the first time, and what I experienced was incredible, like some warm comforting blanket had been thrown around me. In fact, the last time I had felt this comforted was when snuggled up in the hand of my Beast.

"Fitzwilliam," I muttered, testing the name myself, and whispering it on my tongue, seeing how well it fit there. But then something in me said that this wasn't the name I was destined to call him. But as for that voice, well I knew that was one I was most certainly fated to hear speaking my own name, I was convinced of it. But right now, I was

almost desperate to know what his first name would be, but this was nothing compared to the desperation I felt at needing to see him. However, it was a woman's voice that I heard answering him that stopped me from stepping around the corner.

"Oh, my dear Fitzwilliam, look at you here, bringing me flowers again, for they're so beautiful," a woman said, in a fake tone of voice that grated along my nerves enough so that I actually tensed.

"My lady, you are the one who grants me such a gift of beauty, for they are not as beautiful as... and your performance tonight, it was simply... perhaps exquisite is a worthy enough word and I... well, I wanted to tell you, to perhaps ask of you, I mean..." he paused as if needing to take the time to compose himself. It had to be said at this point, the guy wasn't exactly what I would have called a smooth talker... which was another term of my own. But then, I cared little, for I was currently too consumed with another emotion. One that burned inside of me, and was of a raging jealousy and one born solely from hearing him calling another woman beautiful. To such a degree that it had me having to hold myself back from walking around this corner and confronting her. I wanted to face her, tell her he was mine and then gouge her eyes out to prevent her from ever looking at him again!

And this was coming from someone who was not the jealous type.

In fact, I couldn't recall even once ever feeling the emotion before. Which meant this must have been the day for them, for I had never been hit in the heart when hearing a single voice before. Making me now question everything. Had the Fates been right, could this really be him? Could this really be my fated partner in life? It seemed implausible, incredible, and impossible all at the same time. For was it really fated for me to find him that quickly? And if so, how could I be sure?

I also was forced in that moment to look at the facts. I had been dumped back in London, and not ten minutes after opening my eyes I had being chased to a place that I had acted upon without thought, as if actions had just compelled me to be here, right now and out of all of the corridors, out of all of the doors and out of all of the rooms this theatre held, I had chosen my pathway straight to a voice that affected me to the core.

How could any of this be denied?

It could not.

It was him.

And yet, despite knowing this deep down in my heart, it was as if by some cruel twist of fate my meeting him for the first time was when he would be trying to woo another woman. Had the thought not been such a depressing one, I would have laughed at the irony of it all, for here I was trying to search for a fated vessel to be combined with the Beast I loved, and here he was, no doubt trying to convince this woman to love him.

It seemed as if we were both searching for the wrong thing, for I should not just view this as any man who could be connected with the Beast that I loved, but in actual fact, that I would love them both equally so. I knew that now. I knew it as certain as the sun would rise tomorrow.

I knew it the moment I heard his voice.

A voice he was currently bestowing on another.

"Oh, Fitzwilliam, you do me great honour by lavishing me with these gifts. But pray tell me, what is that one that you hold in your hand?" At this I rolled my eyes, and instead of answering her I heard her pathetic girly cry of exhilaration.

"Oh, Fitzwilliam, it's beautiful and it will fit me perfectly for it will match my eyes quite handsomely, do you not think?"

"*No, I do not,*" I muttered, and then moved my lips around as if I was her and acting ridiculous.

"Oh yes… I believe, I think very much so, I mean to say, I think very much so," he said, correcting himself and making me sigh at the sound.

"You are so funny and amuse me greatly," she said, making me roll my eyes and tense, because in my book I wanted to slap her for her reply as it sounded anything but a compliment, for she was clearly laughing at him! It was in this moment I couldn't stand it any longer, I had to take a peek and unfortunately when I did, it offered me very little as he had his back to me.

Although, it was clear that fashion hadn't exactly changed much since my last time here. At least not for the gentlemen anyway. I could see he had taken off his hat, for it hung now in his gloved hand by his side. He also wore a dark green cloak of sorts that was down to his knees. Black boots were worn, no doubt to navigate the cold wet weather and muddy streets. But the only features I could see he personally owned was the flowing, long wavy brown hair. Something that was currently tied back by a black ribbon and even without seeing his face, I was itching to run my fingers through it.

As for the woman, she was still dressed in some Grecian costume, and just as he was about to say something else to her, a man came from around the corner. I quickly pulled down the brim of my hat to conceal my face when he saw me watching the two.

"Hey! You shouldn't be back here!" he shouted out and unfortunately, that meant that my time spying on them was up. But not before I heard the woman gasp dramatically, holding her hand to her mouth. Doing so now as though I was some masked man there to rob them blind!

But I no longer cared about her, for I had finally gained what I needed as she had given it up in her distress. So, I turned around and ran, doing so now with more than just his last name and slight image of his back.

No, for now I had a first name, and one that I was looking forward to calling him...

Adam.

STEPHANIE HUDSON

TWENTY FOUR

A BLOODY WELCOME HOME

"*Adam,*" I whispered the first moment I had chance, finding my back against a wall, placing the tips of my fingers at my lips as I said it.

"Oh Adam… *my Adam,*" I uttered again, adoring the sound it made and feeling my heart flutter because of it. Now all I needed was a face to go with the delectable name. Gods, but I wanted to paint all my body with the name and lie naked waiting for him to find me. I wanted to run to the highest of hills and scream his name to the world, telling all who could hear that he was mine.

But then of course… that wasn't strictly true, for at the

moment, he didn't know me. Not my name, nor my face, but he would. He would… and soon.

I didn't know if Adam had seen me as I ran from the scene, after being chased by a big brute, one who obviously worked behind the stage. However, I knew that at least with a name and place he obviously liked to frequent, I felt confident that I would be able to find him again. But until then, I needed to get out of here and do so without being caught.

So I ran back the way I came, knowing the drunken thugs would be long gone by now. This was confirmed when I burst from the side door and continued running long after the big brute had stopped chasing me. Then, once I felt safe enough to do so, I had leant back against some building I didn't know, which led me to now.

"Adam," I said his name again, if only to offer comfort to myself in place of being wrapped up in my Beast's hand. Then I placed my palms to my slightly bent knees and lowered my head as I panted through everything that had just happened since I found myself back in the mortal realm.

"I found him," I said to myself, hearing my own shock, for quite honestly, I didn't expect it to happen so quickly.

I felt as if I needed a plan of action, yet with no money, no home and not even a place to stay, I felt as if I was staring at the future with little clue as to what to do next. I also knew that I probably looked no better off than some homeless beggar on the streets in a tatty dress, unkempt hair under a stolen hat and bare feet covered in mud and dirt and the Gods only knew what else.

It was in that moment that I was actually thankful he hadn't seen me, for it was not as though I would have made a good first impression. Not in the slightest. In truth, I used to be good at this. I used to be good at taking care of myself. Street Savvy I had called it. Hell, I used to be a damn good thief when the time was needed for it. But right now, knowing that eighty years had passed, well it almost felt as though I had lost my touch with the mortal world completely. I felt lost as if I didn't know what to do anymore, whereas at one time I would have been confident in my ability to survive. It came to something when Hell was easier to live in than that of London!

Well, one thing was for sure, I knew I couldn't just wait around here for much longer, and the last thing I wanted to do now was chance going back to the theatre and bumping into who I now knew was my fated one. Not looking the way I did.

Which meant that it was in this moment when I had convinced myself things could not get any worse, that my stomach started to rumble loud enough that it echoed. I never believed it possible after eighty years of eating the same thing day in day out, that I would ever miss the sight of a Mongolian death worm, let alone the taste. I think if I was to be truthful, it was more who I got to share my meals with that I missed, and right now, I couldn't help but wonder how much pain he was in without me there? How crazed he would be as he searched for me, destroying everything in his path.

I questioned, was he waiting for me to cry out for him like the last time it happened? Would he stop every now and again just to listen and strain his ears? Would he be patting his chest communicating his pain the only way he knew how?

Gods, but it was heart-breaking to think of.

"Abaddon." This time I whispered a different name, and one I loved to Hell and back. One that I missed with every beat of my heart. Which was why it was in this moment that I slumped down in the dirt. Landing on my backside and no longer caring if I got muddy, and no

longer caring that it had started to rain, for if anything, all it managed to do was wash away my tears. Big fat hopeless tears that rolled down my cold cheeks and fell from my chin to my lap.

Ever since this nightmare had begun and Lucifer had turned up to take me, it seemed like it was one thing after another, and bad news just followed even more bad news. Ironically, the only light I had seen was a beacon of hope in hearing that voice, one that even now I could not get out of my head.

I found myself questioning what the sound of my name would be like coming from his lips. He had seemed so unsure of himself, almost stumbling his way through the conversation, when even I knew it should never be like that. It was clear he did not feel comfortable around her, and perhaps being enamoured by her was just an illusion of the heart.

Either way, I would stop at nothing until I made Adam mine. Even his name felt close to Abaddon, as if it was not only me he was fated to be with, but also the beast himself. For the three of us were made to be together, a trifactor that would live throughout the ages of eternity together.

One that I hoped started soon.

It was in this moment that I stood up, deciding enough was enough and feeling sorry for myself in the rain wasn't going to help my situation. So, I took one step away from the wall, and made it all of two more steps when I suddenly realised that my troubles hadn't yet finished. I knew this the moment I felt a rope go around my neck and I was yanked backwards.

"You are gonna pay, bitch, and this time I am going to fuck you then slit your throat!" The big guy was back and as I struggled, I was hit from the front, this time by shorty. I felt the pain as a rib broke from the force and I coughed my way through the agony. Then I was forced backwards, this time further down into a darker alley and one further away from the tavern.

After this, my legs were kicked out at the knees, and I fell down just like they wanted me to.

"I will fucking kill you all!" I shouted before being punched in the face, knocking my face side on into the mud.

"That shut the bitch up!" someone said.

"Jimmy, go and guard the entrance," the guy behind me said, who currently had his knee holding me down digging painfully into my back.

"Yeah, yeah, fucking always last," Beanpole grumbled, walking off and snatching up his hat from the floor where it had fallen from my head when attacked.

I was suddenly pushed down face first in the mud as I felt the first man mount me from behind and start fumbling with my skirt. Of course, this drove me crazy, and I started to buck like a wild animal.

"Fucking hold this cunt!" he grunted with the effort of trying to hold me still. This was when Toothy got in on the action and put a foot on one of my shoulders. So, I turned quickly, making it slip and the second I could get close enough, I bit his ankle making him scream as I came away with a bloody chunk. Then as he howled, I fought back, kicking out behind me.

"The bitch fucking bit me! Took a piece of me! I will fucking kill her!" Toothy shouted, making the big guy behind grab him and say,

"Not until I have felt her squirming on my cock, for I like fuckin' 'em alive."

"Yeah, let's see how you like it when I bite your fucking cock off!" I snarled, making him punch me in the face, and this time hard enough that it made a ringing sound in my ears. I was usually good at fighting, but then four on one, with a fucking noose around my neck… well, it didn't exactly make this an easy fight and in truth, I was definitely out of practise.

But then, just before I was violated in the worst way any living creature could be, everything around me suddenly became deathly still, as if there was a predator watching the whole scene and waiting to make his move.

Waiting to kill.

Gods, but I could even scent the threat of my own kind.

I knew this for certain because it was just something in the air that said the hand of death was here and well…

The humans knew it too.

"Did you hear that?" Shorty said, now looking round frantically and trying to find the source of the demonic growl that echoed between the two buildings.

"Yeah, so what… it just sounds like a dog growling," the big bastard behind me said as he tried to tear my skirt open.

"It would have to be a bloody big dog! Sounded fucking huge!" Shorty said, whilst Toothy was trying to wrap the missing piece of flesh I had spat out on the floor.

"I don't like the feeling of this," Shorty added, making Toothy agree.

"Me neither, and my leg really hurts," he whined.

"Well, I like the feeling of this and I'm going to have it on my cock!" the bastard said, and in my anger now that I was not being held down by two of them, I spun quickly and managed to kick out hard enough that it landed in his gut, knocking the wind from him. Then I quickly scrambled to my feet ready for him.

"Come on! You want to fuck with something, then I will give you something to fuck with!" I said, this time trying to do something I had never managed before. In fact, when I spoke of secrets and how everyone had one… well I had the biggest and most shameful one of all…

I was an Imp without any powers.

Oh sure, I could communicate with smaller beings and had all the usual enhanced attributes my kind did; hearing, strength and speed but at my core I was broken. I had been broken since the very day I was born.

Born on the wrong side of destiny.

But despite this, I wouldn't go down without a fight. Because I was far from weak. So, I tried to harness the anger and use it. Hold it inside of me as I had once heard Pan saying that's what others do. Not that this had been for my benefit at the time, because I realised by the end that he had picked me because I had been weak. Because he had considered me easy prey. Convinced me that I was feeble and needed looking after. But he had been wrong!

And now it was time to prove that, not to him but to myself! So just as the bastard finally managed to catch his breath he rose up from where I had hit him. Then just as he started to come for me, I felt my anger spark. It was small but it was enough that when I punched him, the force was enough to knock him flying on his ass in the mud.

"COME ON, YOU BASTARDS!" I then roared at them, but it wasn't me they were concerned with… as the snarled growls of anger had been getting closer.

This was when I saw the glint of the weapon the bastard pulled, as now he was armed with a blade, and he was coming right for me. But then, I soon realised I wasn't without help as Shorty screamed, the sound echoing behind us. I whipped around just in time to see his silhouette being snatched from the night… just like that.

Gone.

"What the fuck was that?!" Toothy said, now backing away from the entrance to the alleyway where Beanpole had been on guard duty checking for any witnesses. But that was the thing, now he was… *gone too.*

Another scream was heard before a gurgling sound, one sickening enough to know what it was. Even if you weren't of the supernatural variety, there was no mistaking that noise.

The sound of someone being eaten.

It made me question if this was the help I was supposed to receive like Asmodeus had claimed. Well, I was soon to find out, as the next scream came from behind us as Toothy had tried to get away. Both myself and the bastard turned to see him disappearing through the night and this time... *it was from above.* He had been snatched in a mere second, and I knew the only thing that could have done that was a supernatural being that had wings. In fact, I could hear them ever so slightly, knowing that the mortals would have no chance at this.

"I'm getting out of here!" This came from the bastard and the one I wanted to kill the most. So, as he ran towards the alley entrance, I tripped him up with my foot, making him fall face down in the mud where he had forced me down.

Then he looked up in horror to see a shadow travelling at speeds that would have been barely noticeable to the human eye, for it would have looked like a phantom. He got back up and clutched his knife in front of him in a shaky hand as he backed up, giving up on escaping towards the street.

This was when whoever was killing these guys off started to toy with them, as suddenly he dropped a now dead and broken Toothy from above.

"AH!" The last guy standing shouted in fright and then, as he stumbled back, the shadow of death suddenly snatched it up again and tossed it. But because it was too fast for mortal eyes to witness as they were not capable of tracking such a thing, it meant only one thing… the body had just vanished.

Vanished into thin air, with no explanation other than by the Devil himself.

This is when the bastard behind me kicked me to the ground, taking me by surprise. And before I could fight, he held me down in the mud as the rain continued all around us. Held there by a shaking blade to my back. Then he stated in a fearful tone,

"I will kill her! Don't come any closer or she's dead!" This might have been a viable threat if what he faced now had been a mortal just like him. But he wasn't, and I was soon to learn that actually what he faced was one of the most powerful beings on Earth.

A shadow finally emerged down the alleyway that was barely lit by the moon. The shadow of a man, that started to walk closer until I could feel the tip of the blade in my back.

"Don't come any closer or I will do it! I will gut this bitch, I swear to Christ!" At this, we both heard a chuckle before a stern voice in the dark spoke, cutting through the night like this blade could cut through my skin.

"Christ hasn't done much for me lately, so go ahead and see what type of death it gets you." I gasped out in pain as the blade started to press into my skin and the moment I did, I saw two glowing eyes in the darkness… two eyes…

Burning crimson.

A second later, and all I saw was a flash of darkness and suddenly the blade was gone… and so was the man. His scream was the last thing I heard until the alleyway went deathly silent, with only the sound of the rain landing in puddles around me and the sound of my own panting breath. Then, after long moments, I tried to push myself up from the ground, thinking my saviour had gone.

But this was when a voice filled the void…

"I have to confess, I thought you would be more

impressive," the arrogant tone of a man spoke, making me lift my head toward where I heard the sound. This was when I quickly found him leaning casually back against one of the buildings, with his arms crossed, and his ankles doing the same.

He had just killed four men in minutes, quite possibly eating parts of one, and here he was now looking the very epitome of relaxed. I swallowed hard and asked,

"Are you going to kill me too?" At this, I saw the flash of white and red as he smiled, one that was bloody.

"No, darling, I am not here to kill you."

"Then what do you want with me?" I asked, now terrified for another reason. At this he licked his lips and smirked down at me, before telling me,

"It's simple... I am here to welcome you home, little Imp." So he was the one who had come to meet me. He was the help Asmodeus had his son, the King, send.

"And this?" I asked, nodding to the dead I could now see piled up in a broken heap, realising this was what he had been doing in those few seconds I had been trying to get to my feet... unsuccessfully, I might add as I was still having this conversation lying with my belly in the mud.

"This... well this was just an added benefit to finding

you," he said, as he raised one hand to his lips before he started licking his fingers that I could see were still covered in the blood of his victims.

That was when I knew exactly what he was.

"Vampire," I whispered, and he scoffed a laugh, before pushing from the wall and walking over to me. Then, with one hand gripping the back of my dress, he lifted me straight off the floor from the mud and set me back on my feet. A pair that was too unsteady, so he pushed me against the wall and held me there until I was ready.

This was when I saw his crimson eyes glowing for a second time, eyes that were set in the hard lines of a handsome face.

Then he told me,

"Not just any Vampire, darling..." he paused before getting closer to my face, one that he had to bend his neck down so he could reach my small stature. Then, when he was close enough I could have licked the dripping blood from his face, he told me the shocking truth...

"...I'm Lucius, the King of Vampires..."

The End of Book 1
To be continued
In…

Beast and the Imp
Shadow Imp Series
Book 2

ACKNOWLEDGEMENTS

Well first and foremost my love goes out to all the people who deserve the most thanks and are the wonderful people that keep me going day to day. But most importantly they are the ones that allow me to continue living out my dreams and keep writing my stories for the world to hopefully enjoy... These people are of course YOU! Words will never be able to express the full amount of love I have for you guys. Your support is never ending. Your trust in me and the story is never failing. But more than that, your love for me and all who you consider your 'Afterlife family' is to be commended, treasured and admired. Thank you just doesn't seem enough, so one day I hope to meet you all and buy you all a drink! ;)

To my family... To my amazing mother, who has believed in me from the very beginning and doesn't believe that something great should be hidden from the world. I would like to thank you for all the hard work you put into my books and the endless hours spent caring about my words and making sure it is the best it can be for everyone to enjoy. You make Afterlife shine. To my wonderful crazy father who is and always has been my hero in life. Your strength astonishes me, even to this day and the love and care you hold for your family is a gift you give to the Hudson name. And last but not least, to the man that I consider my soul mate. The man who taught me about real love and makes me not only want to be a better person but makes me feel I am too. The amount of support you have given me since we met has been incredible and the greatest feeling was finding out you wanted to spend the rest of your life with me when you asked me to marry you.

All my love to my dear husband and my own personal Draven... Mr Blake Hudson.

Another personal thank you goes to my dear friend Caroline Fairbairn and her wonderful family that have embraced my brand of crazy into their lives and given it a hug when most needed.

For their friendship I will forever be eternally grateful.

I would also like to mention Claire Boyle my wonderful PA, who without a doubt, keeps me sane and constantly smiling through all the chaos which is my life ;) And a loving mention goes to Lisa Jane for always giving me a giggle and scaring me to death with all her count down pictures lol ;)

IMP AND THE BEAST

Thank you for all your hard work and devotion to the saga and myself. And always going that extra mile, pushing Afterlife into the spotlight you think it deserves. Basically helping me achieve my secret goal of world domination one day...evil laugh time... Mwahaha! Joking of course ;)

As before, a big shout has to go to all my wonderful fans who make it their mission to spread the Afterlife word and always go the extra mile. I love you all x

ABOUT THE AUTHOR

Stephanie Hudson has dreamed of being a writer ever since her obsession with reading books at an early age. What first became a quest to overcome the boundaries set against her in the form of dyslexia has turned into a life's dream. She first started writing in the form of poetry and soon found a taste for horror and romance. Afterlife is her first book in the series of twelve, with the story of Keira and Draven becoming ever more complicated in a world that sets them miles apart.

When not writing, Stephanie enjoys spending time with her loving family and friends, chatting for hours with her biggest fan, her sister Cathy who is utterly obsessed with one gorgeous Dominic Draven. And of course, spending as much time with her supportive partner and personal muse, Blake who is there for her no matter what.

Author's words.

My love and devotion is to all my wonderful fans that keep me going into the wee hours of the night but foremost to my wonderful daughter Ava...who yes, is named after a cool, kick-ass, Demonic bird and my sons, Jack, who is a little hero and Baby Halen, who yes, keeps me up at night but it's okay because he is named after a Guitar legend!

Keep updated with all new release news & more on my website www.afterlifesaga.com

Never miss out, sign up to the mailing list at the website.

Also, please feel free to join myself and other Dravenites on my Facebook group Afterlife Saga Official Fan

Interact with me and other fans. Can't wait to see you there!

ALSO BY
STEPHANIE HUDSON

Afterlife Saga

Afterlife

The Two Kings

The Triple Goddess

The Quarter Moon

The Pentagram Child /Part 1

The Pentagram Child /Part 2

The Cult of the Hexad

Sacrifice of the Septimus /Part 1

Sacrifice of the Septimus /Part 2

Blood of the Infinity War

Happy Ever Afterlife /Part 1

Happy Ever Afterlife / Part 2

The Forbidden Chapters

*

Transfusion Saga

Transfusion

Venom of God

Blood of Kings
Rise of Ashes
Map of Sorrows
Tree of Souls
Kingdoms of Hell
Eyes of Crimson
Roots of Rage
Heart of Darkness
Wraith of Fire
Queen of Sins

*

King of Kings
Dravens Afterlife
Dravens Electus

*

Kings of Afterlife
Vincent's Immortal Curse
The Hellbeast King

*

The Shadow Imp Series
Imp and the Beast
Beast and the Imp

*

Afterlife Academy: (Young Adult Series)

The Glass Dagger

The Hells Ring

*

Stephanie Hudson and Blake Hudson

The Devil in Me

OTHER AUTHORS AT HUDSON INDIE INK

Paranormal Romance/Urban Fantasy

Sloane Murphy

Xen Randell

C. L. Monaghan

Sorcha Dawn

Sci-fi/Fantasy

Devin Hanson

Crime/Action

Blake Hudson

Mike Gomes

Contemporary Romance

Gemma Weir

Elodie Colt

Ann B. Harrison